The Culprit

a Florida story

Rich McKee

FIRST EDITION, FEBRUARY 2013

All right reserved. Published in the United States
by Brookside Lit

For information address Rich McKee, Brookside Lit, 1339 Brookside Drive,
Venice, Florida 34285
Cataloging-in-Publication Data

McKee, Rich, 1948--
The Culprit : a Florida story/Rich McKee
p. cm.
1. Florida—Fiction. 2. Everglades (Fla)—Fiction. 4. Environmentalism—Fiction. 5. Education, Higher—Fiction. 6. College professors—Fiction.
I. McKee, Rich II. Title
PS3613.C553C85 2013

ISBN: 1-4818-0645-9
ISBN-13: 978-1481806459

Episodes

acknowledgements: Although the writing of this book proceeded largely in secret, there are a few people who should receive credit or blame for its existence. From an online critique group in which I participated for well over a year there are Laura Albritton and Martha Otis, who were the first to read and offer very sound and helpful comments on the early chapters. Also in on the ground level of perusal and encouragement was my colleague at SCF-Venice, Sheri Chejlyk, as well as my old friend from the undergraduate days, Kenneth Oldfield. On the design, technical, and research ends my wife Linda provided excellent professional advice. As for further inspiration ... that's the easy part: I've taught language and literature for thirty-four years, and have lived in Florida for over twenty of those years.

Surgeons must be careful
When they take the knife!
Underneath their fine incisions
Stirs the culprit, Life!
—Emily Dickinson

I

Mac and the Knife

So you would think that a good teacher, especially a professor, could cast off depression from personal loss, and growing disgust with a profession seemingly up that infamous scatologically-named creek, in a dingy without oars. You would expect him to overcome the throes of understandable funk and misanthropy. Think again.

Strike One: The brain aneurysm that evaporates Sarah in the fall of two years past is of the shock and horror of lightning. One day she is here and happy. Then come the horrendous harbingers—headaches, wrenching neck pain. The next day she is gone. In those tragic rip currents laid on Sean McDuff, her educator hubby, is a forced sabbatical from the little liberal arts college where he works, a half-pay break in large thanks to the rope tricks of one Archibold N.V.S. Goeringthistul, Ph.D., former English Department chairman, and now Associate Vice President of Academic Affairs. He is also the college's first and only Emeritus Professor, but hereafter one whose name must not be spoken in the narrative. A lawyer tells McDuff that he can challenge this gesture of false sympathy (actually a temporary cost cutting move) and win; for McDuff wishes to teach his way through this. To hell with the million dollars or so of trust fund that Sarah received ten years ago from her grandparents, now all his. He doesn't feel he can afford much of anything anyway. Nor is the money anybody's business. Perhaps, he doesn't need to teach, work, whatever, but he wants to. Although Education never quite seems his destiny, his calling, or any of those other bullshit tags put on a poor-paying job, it's just very darn interesting and entertaining sometimes. A grand Globe, Broadway, and Mac is a star, with awards to prove it. So there.

But a few weeks following Sarah's funeral Sean taps out in his e-journal:

When such a thing happens to you so suddenly and with such finality, it naturally and quickly conjures toxins; toxins of the mind, body, and soul that are deadly dementing to you and all you touch. Sarah my whole life's pivot ... gone .... Now I know why seemingly sane and happy people kill themselves, and what horrific hollows life contains. I unlock the closet drawer. The shiny Colt lays there loaded, and smiling it seems. I hold her in my right hand and press the chamber against my cheek, barrel pointing to the ceiling. To my shock she feels warm, fondling, and awakens a resolve. Perhaps the"world" ends with a whimper, not a bang, as the douche bags prophesy. I will test this, give it some leash.

Strike Two: Once upon a day in the late summer of 2011, Sean Millington McDuff, born of Americanized, fourth generation Scotch Irish stock, galumphs from one of those specialized medical facilities, one of those multi-story, sprawling stucco complexes that are the pilot fish to the sharky insurance and medical industries. He drives straight home, in record time, and beelines to his rec room bar. Still sadly single, and no pets, he is in flickering Limbo. Aah, but since the undergraduate battlegrounds of decades ago he is known for his demonically attractive sense of humor, and a tendency arising from certain recollections that sometimes provides a jolly rush akin to the daffodils of Wordsworth's memory, but not so yellow. It's rather an English prof thing. Thus, all surmise, he's going to be all right some day.

Now of course You here, You have read it in fiction, heard it on the news, or more likely seen the TV dramas or big screen blockbusters: Middle-aged man finds out that he has about a year to live, and since he's not yet too far gone or debilitated, he decides that rather than embrace the later stages of carpé diem and just go off on a forced felicity tour, maybe see places he's never seen, and things like that, he deploys terrible vengeance on a few abominations. For although he thinks he has outgrown real energy-sucking Hate, there are still some things festering in his life that will give him spiritual orgasm if they meet with horrendous and bloody destruction, something that buries the bastards under countless cubic tons of smoking, Hiroshimaic rubble. And McDuff knows people from the other war who can help, who can provide clandestine counsel; for instance Martin Derrida, an old weekend warriors acquaintance whose surname borders on the perfect clue. Then there are those Internet cubbies of today, much more explosive than in the era of Timothy McVeigh and his irritated ilk. Aah Cyberspace. It verily reeks of war gods, Molochs like nothing even the poetaster Ginsberg could imagine barefoot on his grandest high wire. Gadzooks! Oh but the bottom line of lines: Professor McDuff has low double-digit months to go, the last one or two prophesied by The Specialist as a spell uncomfortable.

But for now, back to the rec room bar.

`After a snifter of Zaya, a dark, Guatemalan rum (perhaps the last bottle of such spirits in America because when the distillery moved to Trinidad they changed the recipe to something Dr. McDuff's palate cannot relish) Mac picks up his dark iPhone already several notes into the second movement of Tchaikovsky's Symphony #5 in E minor. It is a ringtone no one recognizes.

"What the fuck, Comrade," he answers, for are not most of us now unwitting socialists?

"Hey, professor of the year, what's new?" the good friend, Nash, asks from a thousand miles north. Terribly straight answers follow the query, verbal volleys of surprise, forced laughter, choked sentences randomly uttered, the occasional "Holy Christ Mac, I don't know what to say," and the barely fashionable grace under pressure "What the hell, man, it's life."

"And why won't you consider the surgery, even though it's a slim chance? Tell me again buddy."

"Nash my good man, and favorite pugilist, I've just fucking seen enough. I can't say honestly that I like what I do as much as I did before Sarah died. I guess I'm still good at it. There are some things I'd like to change at the college, sure. I think I still miss Sarah too much, and I'm just fucked up, and tired of it all." He can feel the tremors again, the watery eyes, some faint rumbles of anger.

"Well, what say I just fly down there and knock some sense into you."

2
Pirates and Maidens

Strike Three Looking: Gripeness is all. In early December, at the last department meeting of the fall semester, Mavis Kellpps, Ph.D., feigns biting her tongue, while the bedresssuited Emeritus Professor and Associate Vice President of Academic Affairs across the board table from her continues his critique of today's average freshmen.

"They are devoid largely of work ethic. They are ill-read in even the most basic literatures. They cannot think or write well enough to deal with the most rudimentary of analytical processes; and they are rude and disrespectful. I have lost count of how many times, in the English Novel course I have volunteered to teach once per academic year, that I have had to ask a student to cease and desist using his/her electronic devices during class, to stop "texting" (he employs ye olde finger quotes here), to turn off their damned ringers. It is very disturbing."

Although many years past legal retirement age, EP feels his presence at meetings of his old department is necessary quality control, paramount, another strategy that shall keep the coyotes from the lecture hall. He is the lingering loon on the great lake of winter.

Mac grins that ironical shade of empathy he needs for special discourse such as this. "Yes, Doctor. The student code of conduct is being largely ignored. The college must act." Then he nods to acknowledge Mavis.

She adds/suggests, "I don't see why the college cannot have students deposit their cell phones in a box outside of class. Forbid them to bring them into the classroom. They should be forced to leave their devices outside the classroom."

"You know," Mac smiles wisely, "it has not been so long ago that men were required to check their guns at the door of the saloon. And while we're at it, I suppose we should take the students' guns as well. It's just the safe thing to do."

"What!" Barry Hope, an instructor and elsewhere doctoral candidate, interjects nervously. "Are you serious?"

"Absolutely, Barry," Chairman McDuff shoots back. "Textbooks, notebooks, and pens should be the only acceptable fare for classroom activities; although, if a student has asthma and needs an inhaler, well, I suppose we can make medical exceptions." And by the way, colleagues, did I tell you I have a terminal condition and should be dead by this time next year? Oh, sorry.

"No, I mean ... how do you know we have students carrying guns to class? My god, McDuff, is this really going on? I mean, how long before we have another Columbine right here in our own backyard?" Barry knows that Sean is jerking around the senior decrepits of the department, but cannot resist tossing more coal into the boiler of the runaway locomotive.

"Campus," the Emeritus prof corrects in a scolding tone. "In addition, Columbine is a high school. You can at least dignify your analogy with a logical comparison, Virginia Tech, for example." He turns and stares out the window at the rustling live oaks, where a gray squirrel seems to chatter in agreement.

"Barry, let's just say I have on occasion noticed suspicious bulges in the frontal hip areas of a few rough-looking males in my survey courses, under their black and gray t-shirts, and I doubt they are carrying Bibles."

"Holy shit, that's just as dangerous," shouts Hope Rollins, the new hire from Amherst.

After such a cotillion the reluctant Chair often stops (having had to table the agenda item about raising test score standards for weaseling out of the freshman composition sequence... again) at Fungoola Fred's, for two cocktails and chicken nachos, side of ice water. Barry Hope sometimes joins him. Sean McDuff now, in the safety of his home bar, recalls one especially bright session with Barry about nine months ago, prior death sentence. McDuff, the accidental mentor of the young instructor, is pleased that young Hope can see through so much of his Chair's relentless satire and darkling humor, and more importantly perhaps, sympathize. Better still, Barry is not prone to blather on college matters when off duty.

"I still have a couple of those old wooden flatfish, the SPS surface lures, that my grandfather gave me, and goddamn they drive smallmouths crazy during the summer season, although my smallmouth fishing is limited, now that I work down here on the edge of the Everglades. And you know, Doctor, I still think the largemouth bass is over-rated, both as a fighter and a meal. Fuck these crackers and TV anglers." During Barry's summer month off he returns to his family in northern West Virginia and fishes the streams and cool lakes of his upbringing.

Mac sips his Pyrat on the rocks and nods. "When I was a teenager in western PA, I remember using flatfish a lot, all different sizes, topwater and underwater. There was something about their wobble, and their dangling, their modestly arousing penile shape that took my mind off of how many fish I was not catching. I guess they struck me as borderline porn, something most teenage males are just drawn to, you know. Something sinister too, Freudian, in a subconscious way, don't you think professor?"

Barry spits and laughs, spraying half of his mouthful of Newcastle into his lobster bisque. "Goddamnit, Mac! Why do you have to turn almost everything into something masturbatory?" Barry's stealthy digression now meets with backfire.

"It's not me, really. It's just that when you spend two hours trying to make sense and purpose out of all the bullshit our jack-off colleagues see as the keys to higher education, well, it's hard to pull yourself out of the bog of baloney for several hours following. It's mild perversion therapy or something. You'll see." Mac shakes his head slowly, sadly. He smiles and continues, "I get so pissed when nothing of substance goes down at these meetings, which is to say every time. Most of our distinguished colleagues are so full of themselves, just a gaggle of posturing blowhards, most of them are. Ms. Rollins is an exception, and you have the right idea, and the perfect surname. By the way, you know if you, by some quirk of fate and fortune, date her and then marry her she will become Hope Hope." McDuff extends his arms, palms open and up, as if opening happy hour to the Sacraments.

Barry Hope laughs and shakes his head now, chuckles and adds, "Thank you, sir, for that stirring vote of confidence."

Mac finishes his glass of rum, breathes deeply, then continues, "I took the chairperson job about five years ago, a year before we hired you. But the core majority has not gone away, despite adding some fresh energy like you and Hope Rollins." He runs his fingers over his right eyebrow. "Well, when I'd come home from a typical clusterfuck like this last one, Sarah could sense my über-chagrin, and instead of the stereotypical gee-honey-tell-me-all-about-it shit, she'd take my hand and pull me off to the bedroom."

McDuff balances near the mystically tearful for an instant, orders a nightcap Pyrat. Barry looks away because suddenly, albeit for only a second, here is a Sean he does not know so well, the yet grieving widower. But he quickly turns back to face Mac with a nod, an affirmation bob that says Fuckin'A, dude.

"Maybe I need a girlfriend," Mac wonders aloud.

Barry Hope chuckles, and in a voice carbon copy of Sean McDuff tells his older friend that maybe he just needs "… to get a life."

Indeed, muses Mac, still perched in-house in real time. To get a life. I'm goddamn dead, sooner than later. I could have done it after Sarah died. Now I don't have to kill myself. Some damn alien enemy raging bad-boy growth is doing it for me. The Specialist still says some surgery could slow it down. Fuck that. Hell, I've been dead for a while anyway. "Maybe I need a dog to bleed on at times like this. They just listen." But raising his voice is no relief. He tells himself silently … get a life, a mantra soaked in unstable irony. Actually … I think I need to get another rod and reel, blow off a week of classes, and go up the river. The new outfit will have to be Shakespeare brand. After all, I am a lit teacher, professor, whatever, although it might be more politically correct here in Florida to be seen with a Garcia. I wonder if it's still Garcia Mitchell though. They're very good.

Fishing. Why do we still call it that, he further queries The Vapours. Most of the time spent doing it is devoid of actual fish on the line, in the boat, on the bank, wherever. It's more or less fish hunting, and we don't call duck hunting *ducking,* unless you're doing it with Dick Cheney. What gives with gerunds these days anyway?

McDuff goes for the daffodils again ... backflashes to one of his most-read rants collection of the late 90s, the one about the lure and lore of fishing. *The Compleat Masochist* he titled it, a bit after the very dead Limey's work, but with a dash of insight stolen from the modern novelist Thomas McGuane, Jimmy Buffett's Key West roommate of the 60s. Praise Margaritaville.

"What gives fishing its allure," he spouts to his adorable wife one Sunday afternoon during a late 90s summer, "is not the fish you catch but the great chunks of time you devote to trying to catch the slimy critters. Because without the dominating famine, you could not savor so much the miniscule booty."

Sarah looks up from her book review as a wise and ornery grin takes charge.

"It's the hours, weeks, months and years of wading, trolling, casting that define the sport," Mac continues, looking down at the manuscript. "The Catch is mere punctuation, a scarce, floppy end mark, as rare as a period in the last forty-five pages of *Ulysses.* So you see, dearest, the wide and wet gulf between effort and reward, the many agonies of defeat ... those are what enable and magnify the atypical highs, the occasional joy of landing a fish. Yep, you have to spend a lot of time splashing around with futility if you want to savor victory ... Satisfaction! Where's the soundtrack? Cue the Rolling Stones here. Right love?"

Sarah gets up from the sofa and removes her tank top and bra, her curvaceous ivory torso cuddles Mac's face now.

"You can make the darnedest things amatory," she whispers.

"And you," he replies, "you are so deliciously to blame."

3
Radiant Melancholy

Over the years, in the classroom, one of Sean's favorite fun rants is his background sermon on the scientific and spiritual storms that foster The Victorian Dilemma. The lecture includes a sinkerball overview of Malthus and his *An Essay on the Principles of Population*. Darwin, the usual person of interest in this science versus churches mess, and generally rampant pessimism, is too easy to finger as the only culprit in the decline of the rose-colored eyeglasses in the English nineteenth century. But he certainly helps make the narrative smoke. Many of the students, especially the more religious, have heard about Charles the Bad and his *Origins of Feces* anyway. He sucks big time, they say.

"But Thomas Malthus, an economist and earlier contributor to the collective angst," McDuff tells them, "is a profound and simple pessimist, in essence preaching that human population growth is the root of all evil on the planet. Twentieth Century environmentalism picks up the ball and darts with it, comparing humanity to a cancer that must be put into remission, or the Earth will die." The very few budding environmentalists on board perk up.

"People equal pollution, life-sucking pollution. Nevermind the fact that food supply has and never will be able to keep up with all of humanity's needs. Too much of the earth is starving, and it gets worse with every generation. Think about it."

"Malthus," McDuff adds and stirs, "believes so strongly in his research that he flatly refuses to donate to charities, claiming that they are bad because they invariably support and encourage further population growth." Said sparse tree huggers are sitting erect and grinning now. But this concluding footnote only raises a field of clueless, wide-eyed stares from the majority, much like that of an utterly dumbfounded crowd from a *South Park* scene.

Fate grins at the darnedest times. After one such lecture discussion during the home stretch of fall semester of 2011 in his British lit survey, the doctor is approached following class by a second-time student, Jane K. Green, who always sits tall in the back of the classroom where she takes notes diligently, unbelievably, each day, but never comments except to offer an occasional approving smile. Sean notices for the first time that Jane's eyes are eerily reminiscent of his departed Sarah's Gaia green ones, but less quickly arresting due to her exquisite and lightly bronzed cheekbones. And there's Jane's very long, straight and silky black hair. Plus Jane is probably six feet tall. Sarah five five.

"Doctor McDuff," she says, "do you have a minute?"

"Of course, Ms.Green." Oh shit the weeds, he braces himself. Please Jesus don't be one of those ticked-off god geeks bent on putting Satan's minion in his place. Maybe I should have left out the Darwin publicity.

"I just want to say, and believe me I'm not trying to brown-nose, that your class today really helps me get some things into better focus."

"Why thank you, Jane. But how is that? If I've made an Agnostic out of you, please promise me you won't tell anyone where you got it."

She chuckles. She gets it.

"I promise. But what I mean is ... well, I come from a large family by most standards. Five siblings and a working class mom and dad, well, dad just sort of. You can probably imagine."

"Yes." McDuff's tickle of nervousness retreats.

"Anyway, when I was struggling through high school, I realized that the only way I can do any better is by trying to go to college. But I was a solid B student. And my folks ... well, you know."

"Yes, I get it." Sean McDuff has been there.

"So that's a big part of why I joined the Air Force for six years, almost right out of high school. And that's why I'm able to afford finally to be here." She takes a deep sigh. "So from what I learned today, combined with my personal history, I don't want to have a family, ever. I hope I can convince others some day to consider the same, at the risk of sounding Chinese communist or something."

I'll be god-diddly-damned, Sean thinks. Here's a young woman who can pick through the junk food and come out with a real diet. She could be a trophy catch in the ponderous pond of minnows and crayfish ... and a woman who might induce mixed metaphors like nobody's listening.

"Well, Jane, keep in mind that if you add a smart husband to your life, and you of course are no dummy, then maybe one more intelligent kid won't hurt. The odds are with you." Hmmm, Mac rumbles to himself ... why didn't I think of that when Sarah was fertile and willing?

She smiles brightly now. Then her face settles into a pensive pause. "That won't happen in this town. I have a game plan for many years down the road."

"Graduate school maybe?" McDuff is shivering in old energy, but suspicious as to why he's suddenly sucked into something that is none of his business. Is it *hamartia?*

"That's part of it, if I'm good enough and can get in." She looks away, as if embarrassed to confess this.

"Well Jane, from what I've seen, you are good enough. And if there's any advice or help I might offer just say so, ask, whatever." The offer surprises Sean McDuff, as if something lost and wayward suddenly zips up out of his soul and flies out his mouth before Cynicism can choke it.

Jane Green blushes it seems, looks down, then smiles and faces him. "Thank you, Dr. McDuff. I'll remember you said that too. In another semester or so ... well, we'll see." She extends her right hand. McDuff takes it softly and, then cups his left hand over the brief harmony. He is startled for a second by the otherworldly strength and softness of her grip. He recalls that Earth Day afternoon, a decade ago, when he was allowed to pet the tame Florida panther at the state park, when that rush of radiant melancholy came over him, and he shivered before the great Scream of nature.

In the ides of December, and the very last day of exam week, Sean is called to the office of the Associate Vice President of Academic Affairs for "a chat," as memos will phrase it. It's an appointment that most colleagues will approach with reluctance and caution, the timing being so close to the season of brotherly love and world peace, but having the potential to drizzle acid rain on their holidays. To Sean, though, no man of the clichéd spiritual, stripped of solid happiness and love, and with a still-secret ticket to Oblivion, which may be just around the corner, it's just a temporary upper for his descending spirit.

"As you must know, Dr. McDuff, I will be meeting next semester with our board of trustees to review the college's recommendations for faculty promotions." The EP, in his usual three-piece brownish suit grins across his large desk at Sean, a grin that spawns uneasiness in most college personnel, but only brings out odd energy in McDuff. EP was the English Department chair immediately before Sean, for fifteen years. But rather than take an early retirement, he somehow finagles a new administrative position out of the college, Associate Vice President of Academic Affairs, and continues his rain of surly terror and old fartness. Today he looks more portly and balding than usual, and it appears he's trimmed the gray hairs that grow out of the mole above his left eyebrow.

"Oh, yes, Mr. Vice President, an affair to which you should duly look forward."

The VP nods. "Now I want to ask you about one of your faculty members who is up for promotion to Assistant Professor, and who has been approved by the faculty review committee and yourself, one Mr. Barry L. Hope, a Ph.D. candidate at Florida State who is still ABD."

Sean wonders, why the "one Mr. Barry L. Hope," as if EP is not familiar with him, even though he's sat in on department meetings regularly for four years, and Barry has been at every one. This is foreboding. McDuff simply bows his head slightly in acknowledgment.

"Now Doctor McDuff, I see and have read in the promotion folder of Mr. Hope your recommendation, and a glowing one it is ... is it not?

"He's one of our best instructors, a solid contributor to curriculum development, and very active professionally outside of the college community. His student evaluations are outstanding, as well as the peer reviews."

EP waves his right hand as if clearing the room of cigarette smoke, "Yes, yes, Doctor I am aware of the gist of these supporting documents." He slaps closed the folder. "But I shall not mince words with you today, and I will tell you point blank and to your face that I will strongly oppose the motion to promote Mr. Hope at the spring board meeting."

Motion? It's not a motion, Sean wants to say. It's required approval. And state law simply requires the rubber stamp of the trustees. The board cannot deny promotions. It's an internal college decision. Go back to your fuckin' hole under the bridge and take a nap.

Sean directs a surprised and concerned glare at the VP now, although he's not so surprised really, or concerned. He anticipated opposition from this withered, egomaniacal anachronism. But rather than confrontation, McDuff is poised for further inquiry. "Please tell me more, sir, that I might nip any error in its embryonic stage. Some of us who are less experienced, you must know, are sometimes wrong." This ought to be just fuckin' great, he tells himself.

The EP's eagerness to expound now fills the room, and his voice rises. "You know, Dr. McDuff, I conducted a classroom visitation last semester. It was Mr. Hope's American Literature survey course, the Realists through the Post-modernists. Of course I thoroughly reviewed his syllabi, his pedagogies, how he assigns grades, etcetera." Now he rises from his chair and glances at the bookcase to his right, then back to his singular audience. A frown and scowl fill his face. "Now do you know, Doctor, that Mr. Hope requires blogging of his students, and that such electronic-based rigmarole accounts for fifteen percent of their final grades! Blogging, I say! Yet another side effect of the massive garbage dump that constitutes so much of the Internet ... such as ... well, Facelooks, and Tweeters, and god knows what all." He sits back down, as if out of breath.

McDuff struggles to withhold guffaws, and succeeds in maintaining a visage of sympathetic seriousness. He strokes his chin and waxes pensive. "Mr. Vice President, of course I am aware of Mr. Hope's methodology. And with all due respect let me tell you why I approve of his use of electronic media, in small doses, of course."

The administrator now glares at Sean, but Mac continues, "You see, sir, Mr. Hope's students are writing journals in that medium. That is, they are posting their journals on the course web site. And Mr. Hope diligently reads and comments on their work, and even provides suggestions for resubmissions. It's one way of fulfilling the course, and the state mandated, writing requirements. The Gordon Rule, you know. Many younger instructors prefer this option over the more traditional method of collecting notebooks and leafing through the pages. In addition, a lot of our traditional students are usefully experienced in such media, and are more comfortable employing the electronic journal options. I have considered moving to such myself in my survey classes, a way for students to fulfill the exploratory writing component."

Oh for Christ sake, McDuff says to himself, why don't you just tell the asshole to get with the twenty-first century, or drop fucking dead?

The EP shakes his head from side to side as if he has just heard something so lame and ridiculous that he can barely contain derisive shouts and laughter. He glares in clichéd disbelief, or so it seems, at Sean. He looks over again at the bookcase on the right, putting his hand to his lips briefly. Then the EP turns and sits up strangely straight to face McDuff, placing his forearms and hands flat upon his desk. "Doctor ... Doctor McDuff," he struggles now to contain his consuming disappointment that one could sit in his office in respectful disagreement over anything he has said. "Be that as it may, with you. I am not convinced that some members of the board will agree. But there is more," he pauses, "and this has been brought to my attention by one or two distinguished board member who, at least for now, shall remain anonymous. It has much to do with what you allude to as outstanding student evaluations."

Holy crap, McDuff tells himself. A plot. A plan spawned by even bigger idiots, a few of which don't even have any higher education, yet sit on a governing and advisory board for a college. Appointed by the governor, The Ass of Tallahass. It has to be, as Grant Samuels, his cynical colleague in poly-sci often spouts, that education really is seen by most politicians as The Enemy. That the dumber the voters are, the weaker in communication and critical thinking skills, the more likely most of those greedy crooks can get elected, and elected. It's not that there really isn't more money to put in the school and college coffers, but that our twisted government won't put it there and risk attracting higher numbers of quality people to the education profession, more who could make a difference.

Sean says nothing to EP, but widens his eyes to see where this is going now. Hearing is only part of disbelieving.

"Doctor McDuff," the EP/VP begins, as if about to reveal for the first time something newly dug up from the Book of Revelation, "have you heard of an Internet evaluation tool titled RateMyProfessor?"

RateMyProfessor! McDuff is thrown off guard. So that's his game. Sucking up to the new clueless Board. RateMyFuckingProfessor is just another cyberspace popularity contest, no useful evaluative standards. It's widely played with, and sort of fun, but by no means professionally useful. They even have a category to rate a teacher's appearance. *Hot*, or not so. And if a student checks *hot* the prof gets a red chili pepper next to the Easiness rating column. A five-point scale otherwise. No doubt one or two of the board members sees all this as relevant and informative. Can't EP smell his inconsistency here?

"Sir, that's an online and anonymous survey site, of sorts. "

"Indeed it is, Doctor. But you must realize that even the Internet may not be all bad. I am informed by two trustees, whom to my delight have been doing their homework, that Mr. Hope's scores on this evaluation tool are less than glowing."

Probably because he has clear and solid standards and expectations, Sean wants to quip. This lunacy is going nowhere but deeper into the Land of Oz, McDuff tells himself. Even Kansas is more stable, but that too is on the other side of the globe from these people. Just humor the blathering shitferbrains and get out.

Sean nods his head and dawns a quizzical smile.

"Mr. Vice President, I sincerely thank you for this new information. It is surely something that requires my immediate attention." He grips the arms of his chair. "Now if there's nothing more to add, I won't take up more of your time today." Because I fear if I did I'd probably wind up smashing your wrinkled face into your goddamn desk. McDuff rises.

"That will be all Doctor," says the EP with a smile. "And please remember too that ALL instructional personnel are being at least partially evaluated by my watch, on a nearly week to week basis now, even those like yourself who are tenured and awarded administrative positions. Excellence is all. Remember that please sir."

Sean is walking out the door now, but turns to smile back. "Well put, sir. Sometimes we all need such a reminder. Good day. And thank you once again." You totally fraudulent, posturing, wad of possum shit. *Please* in-fucking-deed. *Awarded* administrative positions? McDuff calms himself with a reality check of sorts, a tersely whispered hall monologue: "A dying man with nothing to lose but his life, and yet my self control and melodramatic skills are still sharp, sharp enough that when taunted by a despicable fool, I can resist irrational, unreasonable retaliation ... for now."

But it is the proverbial straw that snaps the camel's spine, one boilermaker too many. By Christmas Mac's rage gurgles quietly, nearly twenty-four seven. Occasional but mild discomfort, as forewarned by The Specialist, crackles through his abdomen and points south. Whether the rarely needed pain meds help is moot, but the acid reflux pills from across the counter provide quick relief. Madness? Sadness? Madness again?

"The system, my life, are going down the crapper." Alone on his back deck overlooking the river, a mug of Guinness in hand, McDuff assesses aloud and loudly his current scenario. His closest neighbors are five miles to the west, so volume is not an issue.

"My college is sinking," he shouts as he sits his mug on the railing and addresses the night river, "and the powers that be are not confronting the crooked fools out of capital city, much less the in-house loads, or the governor's new appointees to the board of trustees ... ignorant motherfuckers and their *business model* ideas on how to run a college. At least three of the dipshits don't even have a college degree! What the hell! They're charged with overseeing higher education, and don't even have a lower one."

"Someone must make a statement, a Scream, if you will (shit, don't go sounding like the EP now) ... the old heads-must-roll trick is in order." A chilly sort of paralysis envelops him from toe tips to the back of his skull. A cold revelation it seems, but comforting as a muse visitation. "I AM the chosen One. I shall go out in a raging blaze of glory, and take a bunch of those bastards with me."

He reaches for the mug of beer, lifts the mug to his lips and takes a refreshing gulp. As if the pin of a monster grenade has been light-speed yanked, a booming strategy ensues: "I always liked bombs, and cars. But I need the explosives ... really major league ones. There is nothing to lose but the losers."

McDuff thinks back, remembers that old acquaintance from the Army Reserves, decades ago ... Martin Derrida, decorated dem-olitionist who, following discharge, now pursues a successful liveli-hood dealing in forbidden military paraphernalia. Sean bought a nice M-16 from him nine years ago. Yes. Why not call the old bomber again, Martin Derrida, marTAN dare-E-DAH, as the lieutenant pre-fers.

Mac goes into his home office and digs out an old personal phone book ... activates iPhone ... dials ... answering machine ... sigh ... Mac leaves a message.

Three days later Martin returns the voicemail. A business ren-dezvous is set. No time to waste.

4
Car For Sale

Martin Derrida, tan sports jacket over navy blue shirt with faded Levis, waits by the southeast watchtower of the Castillo de San Marcos, a very old Spanish fortress, now a national monument overlooking Mantanzas Bay, St. Augustine. It's the day before New Year's Eve. The tourist attraction is but moderately abuzz.

"Good afternoon, lieutenant," McDuff says.

Derrida grins and shakes his hand. In the retired officer's mirrored sunglasses Sean sees himself smiling. "Sergeant," Martin replies. "Very good to see you again. I see your are staying in shape."

"Oh, don't let the thinness fool you. Stress and such help keep the weight off, but I do get a brisk twenty minute walk in four or five times a week. And you look your usual A-plus self." Martin, Sean assesses, must be a few years past the half-century mark by now, but looks very thirtyish, even with the shaved head.

"Spoken like a true professor, McDuff. Thank you." Derrida's visage now moves from salutary to informal business-like. "Let's walk, maybe go across the avenue and have some lunch, on me of course. I believe I can provide useful counsel and technical support for your, uh, cause let's say. But before I forget," he removes a small cell phone from his jacket pocket and puts it in Sean's hand. "After today, any communication between us must take place over this phone only. When deal and/or deed are done, it will become nonfunctional. Or you can just pitch the damn thing. That's an order," he smiles.

McDuff slips the phone in a pocket of his beige cargo pants. The grave and serious tenor of his future begins to enthrall him, a tickling rapture. Am I becoming more nuts by the day, he wonders. And how testiculous am I truly?

They leave the fort, cross A1A, and find a restaurant with a second story deck overlooking the sunny intracoastal waterway. They take a table at a far end of the deck, away from the other diners. After brief small talk, ordering cocktails and grouper sandwiches, Martin takes off his sunglasses and gives Sean a stern glance as he removes an iPad from a small leather carrier. He lays the e-tablet on the table.

"Let me offer some assumptions as to the nature of your present situation, perhaps your mind frame, and of course your brewing plans. Feel free to correct or clarify if you like, but you don't have to."

McDuff nods. Holy friggin' hush puppies, why do I feel like I'm about to be frisked by the CIA?

"Following your voicemail, I did some research on you, your life of the past few years, as I do with all of my clients, and potential ones. Thus the small delay in my return call. From such research I am able to come up with what I think are reliable profiles, both personally and psychologically, and that tells me whether our needs can relate. Now by *needs* I don't mean anything like a partnership, a mutual accord, and so on. I just mean, can I provide the tools for you to succeed in your plans, and more importantly, can I trust you?"

He's still damn impressive, McDuff notes. Sean just nods again, but more deliberately this time.

Derrida takes the gesture as a declaration of faith. "Good. Now I'm sorry to hit on what is still a very raw nerve, but first of all I strongly suspect that, hell I know it, that the very sudden passing of your beloved wife a couple of years ago continues to do your world view no good at all. The Fates fucked you over. And believe me I say that without a tinge of disrespect, and much understanding ... even empathy, sergeant. Enough said there."

But he did hit a nerve hard, and McDuff reflexively rubs an eye.

"I assume you wish to take out quite a few people whom you dislike, or disapprove of, and probably yourself with them, since you are diagnosed with a terminal condition."

McDuff's jaw goes limp. He gains control, then stammers, "How the hell ... what the ... shit Martin, how the hell do you know that? I've told absolutely no one. Well, only one person, but he's a thousand miles away and sworn to secrecy. Do you work for the fuckin' clinic too?"

Derrida's calm is as the eye of the storm. "I told you, I do significant research. And my connections are thorough. Some are in fact CIA moonlighters with extensive computer hacking skills. That's all I will tell you except that my research network goes well beyond military data bases."

"So doesn't a suicidal profile concern you here? Isn't that about as unstable as a client can be? Is that what you take me for?" Sean, very annoyed for an instant, just as quickly falls back into a curious tremor.

Martin Derrida leans forward, glares lightly at McDuff, sips his scotch. He grins a little now. "You are no danger to me or my associates. I mean that with all due respect to you and your situation. It is not some macho intimidation tactic. If I did not trust you and believe you to be a courageous and honorable man, I would not be here."

Martin is grinning now, and goes on, "Sean, I probably know more about you presently, and what makes you tick, than anyone in your life, although that fact is the more plausible because you no longer have any close living relatives. I'm sorry."

Derrida glances to the street below, now bustling with cars and shopping tourists.

McDuff rearranges his thoughts, emotions, sips his Pyrat on ice, takes a deep inhale of the onshore breeze. "You're right Martin. You can trust me. I am damn determined to wake up some motherfuckers, before I go into nap mode forever. You can trust me."

Derrida smiles once more. "Let's cut to the chase, Sean. Within about six weeks I can deliver to you a foolproof weapon that contains enough explosives to obliterate a multiple-story building that covers about a half acre of ground. The best delivery system for this is what is known in the trade as a car bomb. Does this interest you?"

McDuff's face wrinkles with joy, and a little disbelief. "Tell me more. Yes. Yes. I'm interested. Very much."

The lieutenant continues. "The price includes everything you may require, including a state of the arts detonator. You'll receive thorough instructions. You cannot fail."

Sean bobs his head in affirmative approval. "This sounds easier than I imagined. Really. I mean ... well ... please go on."

Derrida turns on the iPad. "I require twenty thousand dollars today, and another twenty thousand at time of delivery, which will be home delivery, unless you wish otherwise. Upon delivery you will be instructed on use, options, all of the possibilities, including cautions, plus general tips for maximum success, efficiency ... you get the picture, or will get it I assure you." He slides the i-Pad across the table to McDuff. "Now look at these models and just tell me which one you like."

The professor's eyes widen in more joyful disbelief, then go into a puzzled focus. He stares at the screen of the i-Pad for a good ten seconds unable to speak. "These are cars, lieutenant."

"Well of course," Martin replies sharply. "You are buying a car bomb. All of them are very reliable and inconspicuous vehicles that have undergone rigorous evaluations, and devious modifications, by my associates. They are as fully equipped as any normal road model ... air conditioning, anti-lock brakes, a decent sound system, even a spare tire ... so as not to arouse suspicion. Not the sort of shit your average radical Discontent drives. But of course they are deadly beyond the wildest dreams of any Detroit engineer." He grins and adds, "Just please don't be a wise ass and ask to see the fucking car fax."

Sean chuckles. Derrida responds with another short smile. McDuff, a bit dumbfounded, finally asks, "How much gas will be in the tank, on delivery?" He hopes Martin will not take his weird curiosity the wrong way.

"It will be at least half full. I hope that's not a deal breaker." The lieutenant begins to laugh a little. He gets it.

Looking over the four pictured vehicles now, the somewhat dying prof gives another nod of approval. A full minute goes by. "I like the red one," he says, "but which would you recommend?"

"That's as good a choice as any really. It's a small Kia van, and especially compatible for your purpose because the storage compartment in the rear where the explosives are packed is easily rigged and insulated, to minimize road vibrations. That means there is almost no chance of the detonation wiring working loose during any transit situation."

Sean scrutinizes the red van image and grins.

"Sold," he says.

"Also," Derrida goes on, "this model has an especially kick-ass sound system compatible with nearly any plug in add-on audio device out there. You can blast your favorite and/or most appropriate music during the drive up, if that's part of your strategy. It's a great apoca-lyptic touch, a wonderfully ominous accent,"

McDuff is all smiles now, in blockbuster mood. He flashes back to *Apocalypse Now* and the Wagner background blarings, "The Ride of the Valkyries," as Colonel Kilgore's helicopter gun ships descend on that outpost Vietnamese village. Fuckin' beautiful, he says to himself, but what tune will it be for me? Damn. More fuckin' deci-sions. But at least that's an aesthetic one.

5
Happy New Year

Sean Millington McDuff goes out for lunch on New Year's Day to a local seafood shack, Poopdecks Incorporated. It's a risky name for a restaurant, he thinks. But it's a legitimate nautical term, Poopdecks. And Poopies serves the best clam chowder and gator bites south of Okeechobee and east of Naples. Not much frequented by college employees or students, it's a safe retreat for a man now gravitating toward the darkly demonic, a budding, murderous madman. There is no one there to ask him why he is paying tens of thousands of dollars for a car bomb that will take out himself and a dozen or so politicians, plus a few lousy college administrators, oops ... and a handful of innocents in the wrong place at the wrong time. No one pries as to why. And not a soul in Poopdecks Inc. will ask him who is going to take over his classes after spring break. Only the waitress asks, "Sir, would you like another beer?"

He ponders briefly and picks at his last floret of broccoli. "Yes," he says. "I'll have one more."

"Dr. McDuff?" A familiar voice queries from a small booth a few spots down from his. A strong but feminine voice.

Instead of the predictable oh-shit-who-is-that, McDuff feels a warm startle. He smiles and turns to see Jane Green rising alone from her booth three down from his. Was she there when I arrived, he wonders. How could I not have seen her?

Jane walks up to his table, smiles and offers a handshake. McDuff takes her hand.

"Well Happy New Year sir."

"Likewise Miss Green." The handshake ends reluctantly it seems. "You're not one of those hungover college students today, are you? You seem alert."

Jane is wearing a red silk skirt cut just below her knees, tan leather jacket over what appears to be a white cotton tank top. Little or no makeup and her long black hair pulled back in a glowing ponytail. She is turning heads, many of them attached to red necks.

"On no sir," she replies quickly. "I spent last night with mother going over the family futures, then turned in early. I'm boring. Never saw the ball drop."

McDuff dawns a grin of skepticism and says, "Don't try to fool your former professor, Miss Green. I'm sure you can celebrate with the best of us if you wish. Not that I raised any hell last night myself. I just took this year's Eve off."

Why the hell am I telling her that, Sean asks himself.

"You too," Jane happily replies. "Yes, I think it feels great not to be nursing an alcohol overdose on January one. It has to be a good sign for the new year, right? You must be planning a killer semester at the college, right?"

Sean almost quips 'If you only knew,' in keeping with his often unbearable ironics. But he laughs through it and says, "Oh the biggest." Suddenly a startling sadness jolts him and he has to look away. He rallies a forced smile and looks her in the eyes again. "What do you have up your sleeves, Jane, college-wise? Are you closing in on graduation?"

A waitress squeezes by Jane and says "Excuse me, ma'am."

Jane glances at her and says, "Sorry."

Nearly without thinking McDuff points to the empty seat across from him and says, "Please sit down if you like, I mean if you're not in a hurry. I'm all ears on holidays."

To his surprise she smiles and sits down quickly.

"Thank you. I will. I mean, I do have a question or two you could help me with ... about grad schools maybe. Not that I need an answer right away." She seems suddenly a little nervous, but strangely determined. She looks down at her gold wristwatch. Then smiles at McDuff.

"Ask anything," he answers. "I've got nowhere to be today but where I want to be." His waitress delivers a bottle of Dogfish Head 90 IPA. "Would you like something to drink, Jane?"

Jane Green seems flustered for an instant, then blurts, "Oh ... OK. Thank you. It can be a small way of making up for last night. Ha ha. Is that what you're up to?"

"Maybe," McDuff laughs. "I never considered it as redemption, but shut me off after this one. Two is my limit anymore, at least when I'm on the road, so to speak." He begins to feel as if they had come to the restaurant together, and just sat down after a fifteen minute wait. Glad I'm not driving a car bomb today, Sean tells himself. The chance meeting almost feels as predestined as his upcoming Armageddon, and a good distraction.

"Ma'am?" the waitress asks.

"Oh," Jane says. She looks at Sean's bottle. "I've been wanting to try that. I'll have what he's drinking."

The waitress smiles and says, " Good choice, ma'am. I'll be right back."

McDuff grins and says to Jane, "If you like a heavy hoppy tasting brew, you won't be disappointed. But it's nine percent alcohol content, so brace yourself."

"My goodness, professor. I'm impressed. You know as much about beer as you do about good literature ... and good writing. " She pauses, then says, "You know, I never told you, but I really liked that second semester freshman comp class of yours a couple of years ago. The one that doubled as an intro to lit. That really got me on track in a lot of ways." Jane stops abruptly it seems, and McDuff intuits that she probably thinks that he thinks that she's just kissing his ass. But he suspects that's not the case, that she's just probably as thankful to have someone to talk with as he is.

"Jane," he smiles, "I remember your work in my classes over the last couple of years. I really do." He really does. "And I think you deserve most of the credit for getting on track, and certainly staying there. You're one of the brightest students I've had in at least a decade."

Maybe if she thinks I'm kissing her ass she'll feel better. It balances out.

"So there, ma'am. We've got the formalities and ice breakers out of the way. Really, how the hell are you doing this first day of twenty twelve?" The vernacular always seems to help with these students, he thinks.

Jane Green gives a thankful sigh, smiles. Just what the doctor ordered. The waitress returns with Jane's beer. Jane smiles again, then pours before the waitress can do so. After a few seconds to allow the foam to peak, she takes a sip, then sits the heavy mug softly back down on the table. She looks at Sean.

"Well, Doctor McDuff, I've narrowed down my choices for grad school, and I'd like to know if you would be interested in writing a letter of reference for me."

Mac is genuinely surprised and happy. "Fantastic, Jane," he enthusiastically replies. "Of course I will. Tell me more please."

"Well, I majored in Humanities and minored in biology, because I was sort of searching, you know?"

McDuff nods and grins. "That's an interesting journey you've been on."

"It sure is," she says. "And I just found out last month that the college is accepting some more credits from my military schooling that will put me on track to graduate in May. I've been busy checking out grad programs in environmental studies."

Sean looks surprised. I didn't see that coming, he tells himself. Jane goes on.

"You know Doctor, I come from a very long line of Floridians, before they were even called Floridians. See, I was born on the old reservation and spent the first ten years of my life there with my really dysfunctional sort of a family." McDuff's eyebrows raise. He never suspected she was a Native American, a Seminole, Muskogee Creek.

"Long story short," Jane continues, "I don't like what's happening out there to nature, and since I'm no billionaire, my best chance to help, to make a difference, is maybe through education, first my education. Does that make sense to you?"

She's a Green in every sense, McDuff observes in impressed silence. A closet environmentalist himself, he feels some old nerves charging. He bailed on activism over twenty years ago when it hit him that unless a truckload of millionaires have your back, you cannot save the environment from the cancers of capitalism gone bad.

He isn't sure that education is the savior, but maybe it can slow the progress of the poison. He nods in affirmation and smiles broadly, clearly pleased with what he hears.

"Jane, can you keep a secret?"

Jane gives him a puzzled, curious smile now. She appears more relaxed. She nods and replies, "Yes I can, Doctor. I know we haven't talked much, but I've listened to you very intently in class, and watched you, your body language. I trust you ... and I respect you ... and, well, I should just shut up and listen again."

She hopes he's not joking, and that the nature of the secret is somewhat personal, but not embarrassing.

McDuff grins and says, "About twenty-five years ago I was very active in Earth First, you know, those very radical green warriors, as the press called us. I spent a year out in Washington and Oregon messing with the big lumber companies, spiking trees, taking out heavy construction, or in their case destruction, equipment ... just doing some major vandalism." He pauses and stares across the room for a few seconds, then turns back to Jane. "I still don't know exactly why I became an English teacher. I suppose ... well, hell I don't know."

Jane looks pleasantly surprised now. Mac continues.

"So what I mean Miss Green, is that I applaud and respect your decision, your direction. And you're right about the education angle. It's our only hope it seems, albeit a slim one. Our society pays lip service only to supporting environmental issues, strengthening its schools, and a lot of other essentials. But if good and bright people like yourself carry on, I guess there's a chance something will eventually work. But be sure to buy lottery tickets every week too. It's also going to take a lot of plain luck." Sean hopes that didn't sound overly preachy, or clichéd.

"Well, I'm not sure I'll go into teaching yet," she adds, laughing softly. "I'm still feeling it all out. Maybe I'll eventually try law school, and specialize in environmental law. My GI bill can take me a long way. I'm glad of that."

McDuff is happy to be in the presence of a younger person, one not as young as most of his students, who has goals, aspirations ... one who is articulate and perceptive, at least about things that once mattered the world to him.

"You know, Jane, it's a no-brainer for me as far as being able to write you a strong letter of recommendation based on your academic work. But if you don't mind, tell me a little about your pre-college years. I know you spent some time in the military. What was it? Seven years? And I assume you attended local high school; and I recall you said you were a B plus student, right?"

Jane takes another long sip of beer, blinks, then a deep breath. She seems reluctant to go there, but nevertheless begins. "I didn't get my diploma until I was nineteen. I was held back twice due to attendance difficulties mostly. Family issues. I think I told you I have five brothers and sisters, three brothers and two sisters, all older than me. Well, two brothers now. One died in a car accident when I was sixteen. My other two brothers are in prison for armed robbery and manslaughter, and will be for a long time. My two sisters are both married and living around Orlando, and they and their husbands all work for Disney. We don't get along or see each other much at all. Dad died the first year I was in the Air Force, when I was twenty-one. He was an alcoholic. Mom lives near Naples in a little condo off Alligator Alley. The family money, what little there still is, comes from one of those Injun souvenir businesses on old Alligator Alley. Mom's OK, but pretty frail now. She's mid seventies. So as you can guess I was a rather late, unplanned offspring." Jane takes another drink of beer and looks away, across the restaurant, as if to gather her breath and energy again. McDuff notices that this is a little unpleasant for her, perhaps annoying. That was quite a bang-bang biography, he tells himself

"My goodness, Jane," he says, "you are indeed a very special sort of survivor. Wonder Woman has nothing on you." That seems to restore her composure a bit, in spite of it being a silly analogy.

"Oh, thank you, Doctor McDuff." She looks at him now and smiles again. "So as you might guess, when I got high school behind me I joined the military about a year later. It was interesting, eye-opening … I wound up working in the Air Force's drone program and, well, a lot of it, most actually, is classified." She shakes her head from side to side and looks down at the table again. "Some of it was pretty crazy, scary stuff, when I think about it. Spent my last two years in Afghanistan."

It seems she cannot find more words, or doesn't wish to. For there are the episodes of sexual harassment that put her on leave a couple of times. Officers, mainly, saying things to her like, "Hey, sweet sergeant, saw your photo in that operations manual. So what's next for you, baby? The *Sports Illustrated* swimsuit issue?" And there were a few failed rape scenes. Then there was the night, the night when she considered mild self-immolation, making some scars on her face and wrists, to keep the boys away. Just as unnerving was the female counselor, Captain Glover, who helped Jane through the trauma of this and that close call, then turned out to be a lonely, pushy lesbian. So for Jane it came down to a contradiction of the Wolfe proverb, you can't go home again. Going home again was her only hope.

It is information McDuff does not need though. His eyes widen and his face takes on a look of sincere interest, respect, a dash of sympathy. Some astonishment hovers too, but it is darkened by personal ghouls peeking around every corner of his mind. He senses that Jane Green, in the last ten years of her challenging life, has run the highway to hell and back, and done so in fairly decent shoes. Only minor damage.

On the other hand, what the fuck does it all matter now?

"Jesus Christ, Jane. I had no idea. You don't need to tell me any more." Now it is he who is somewhat verbally frozen. He places his right hand on the side of his face, elbow resting on the table, and stares and smiles at her.

"I'm sorry," she says.

"No. No. Don't you dare be sorry, damn it. You are a special person, very special. I understand a lot of what you are recounting." Sean feels some anger stirring in his gut, but can not understand why. "Listen, I will write you a reference letter that will get the serious attention of all who read it. Just tell me who to contact. And if you don't get accepted, if you don't get the deal you want, you tell me and I'll go there and knock some sense into them." McDuff quickly feels a little embarrassed. He isn't really going anywhere but up in smoke in less than two or three months. That's a little unprofessional, he tells himself.

But what the fuck does it matter now?

They small-talk another twenty minutes before exiting for the parking lot together. He walks her to her car, some sort of Toyota SUV, and they lightly, reflexively hug good-bye. She says she'll be by his office in a couple of weeks or so with those addresses.

During Mac's drive home from Poopdecks he mulls it all over. He decides that helping Jane Green with her future plans, her education beyond Cypress State College, is a noble and necessary last act.

I almost wish I could be around to see her graduate, maybe get another hug. Ha. But hell, by then I may be bed-ridden and wretched beyond endurance, or even in jail. Another good reason to go down with the ship while I have a chance. I wonder why I haven't really started to feel like hell, except in my fucking attitude, my zeal for dealing a big bloody lesson to those goddamn frauds and politicians. I've really lost it. I don't know how the hell I managed to keep it together tonight with her.

As he turns on to the sandy shell road that winds a hundred yards to his concrete driveway, and the sprawling five thousand square feet ranch style home that he and Sarah built on ten acres of mostly riverfront property, Sean McDuff punches on the car radio. An oldies station out of Fort Myers is piping "Fire and Rain" in to his rim of the Everglades. Sean has not been able to listen to that song for over two years. He turns the radio off.

6
Joy of the Worm

Just three weeks into the semester, McDuff takes a day off to receive the prearranged call of Martin Derrida, noon on Monday, January 30. He tells his secretary he has an appointment with an eye doctor, something about possible cataract surgery. Fabrication it is. His eyes are still fine, but his brain? And with weeks and weeks of sick days in Mac's academic wallet, it will be no loss of pay in spite of what the new college board is trying to change regarding medical leave and benefits.

"Bend over faculty and staff. Here comes the real world," he imagines the trustees shouting to a joyful tune. But in reality, what the hell? The Tubes await Sean anyway. Just let them try to collect, inflict, dock, whatever.

McDuff turns on the plain little black cell phone at the designated time. It rings ten seconds later.

"Good day," he answers.

"Hello McDuff. And how are you feeling on this winter day?" The voice of Derrida sounds cheerful and vibrant. Sean has a mild rush of relief.

"Lieutenant! Good to hear your smiling voice." It eludes McDuff that Martin is asking about his physical condition, that the question is more than rhetorical.

"Well of course it is. Who the hell else would be calling on this phone?"

Sean laughs and says, "Well, I guess you're right, as usual." His fishing for more introductory small talk is snuffed as Martin goes on.

"Delivery in three days sergeant, at two p.m., your home. Please take precautions that there will be no one else there, no deliveries, maintenance people ... you know."

While surprised at the sudden news, McDuff is also excited. Yes, he says to himself. It is coming together. Sweet HeySoos, formerly sweet Jesus.

"McDuff?" Martin says.

"Yes sir."

"Did you copy that?"

"Absolutely Martin. I'm just very happily surprised at your punctuality. It's something I'm not used to seeing much in my line of work. Really, I look forward to seeing you again, and accepting ... delivery."

"Yes. Very good. I will be driving the car personally, followed by one of my associates, who shall remain anonymous. In other words, he will stay in the other car for the half-hour or so it will take me to brief you on operational procedures, dos and don'ts ... some general advice, tips, the usual safety tips. Nothing you can't handle."

"I understand, lieutenant." Sean recalls that there are perplexing instructions regarding payment. "How do you want me to arrange for the final financial installment?"

"No problem there," Martin is quick to answer. "I see you have put the money in the designated investment account, as per my instructions in St. Augustine. The transaction is in progress, and I assure you there are no more hoops to jump through. The money is now in the realm of the untraceable. You are paid up in full, and we thank you."

"Thank you, lieutenant. See you in a couple of days then." McDuff's head is now lightly reeling in disbelief, and it's a very pleasant feeling. "Oh?" he thinks to ask. "Do you need directions to my place?"

There is a short silence. "Are you serious, sergeant?" Derrida then emits a quick ha ha. "I'll take that question as over excitement, since I know that you must know better. It's the anticipation, right?"

Sean laughs back and says, "Aah shit, Martin ... I'm just really surprised ... and psyched I guess too. I'll be clear-headed and focused when you get here, I assure you." Given what McDuff imagines to be the lieutenant's high tech capabilities, his cyberspace sophistication and savvy, his secret service connections ... hell, Sean muses, he probably knows how many tiles in my roof are cracked.

"I'm sure you will, sergeant. So, see you on Ground Hog Day. By the way, you don't have woodchucks in south Florida, do you?"

Now that's an odd question, Sean thinks to himself. Ground Hog Day? Punxsutawney Phil. Wheeling Will, and so on. For woodchucks, McDuff imagines, the sunshine state would be a peninsula of shadow, because nine out of ten February twos are relentlessly sunny; thus nearly always six more weeks of winter and tourist season. Irony and paradox rampant.

"Nevermind," Martin finally says. "See you in a few days."

The cell phone goes silent. McDuff turns it off. He waits a few seconds, then pushes the phone's ON button again. It's dead.

On Thursday Sean of course cancels classes once more to receive delivery of his forty-thousand dollars weapon of moderate mass destruction. It is the first time in his tenure at Cypress State that he has missed two class days in one week for reasons other than professional development, as they call treks to conferences. This time it's a "personal day." The school's board of trustees wants to eliminate such shenanigans, by the governor's not-so-secret orders. It's not effective business, they say. Fuck those motherfuckers, McDuff said to himself months back when he first heard of the trustees' plans. They claim that in the "real world" such random, uncontested mini-vacations (too often taken on the spur of the moment) are bad for the company. What fuckin' company? It's a college.

Also, Mac asks himself, why is it that over the last year and a half or so my vocabulary is more laced with obscenities, such as the f-word and its variants? Goddamn it, anyway.

After a breakfast of eggs, bacon, and wheat toast, McDuff sits down on the back deck that overlooks the Cypress River, laptop in lap. He needs a manifesto ... something that doubles as a suicide note

... a short one ... suitable for email and the op-ed pages ... because most readers today are short on focus. He begins to type:

Dear Cool World,

Why? Why and how does an honored professional suddenly change into a heartless mass murderer? How is it that he of heretofore heroic standards can stoop to such a mindless act of sheer terror? What drives seemingly normal people to commit such evil acts, taking their own lives in the process? What does such a horrible thing prove or accomplish? Although my answers to these questions will no doubt fly over the heads of countless readers, especially the families of the victims of my act, I hope that a few will pause and reflect, re-read this and think, think hard. It is certainly not without some sense of horror and shame that I arrived at my decision to take the lives of people with whom I am in profound philosophical and practical disagreement. Even being aware that my deed must unavoidably and unfortunately kill a few innocent people as well, I believe that in the long run that the wake-up call that the state of Florida and this country needs will eventually ring through the shock of it all. Of course the fact that months ago I was diagnosed with a terminal illness, and that about two years prior to this my loving wife died suddenly and unexpectedly, made the fatal decision much easier to gravitate toward. But save your sympathy. In short, much of my frustration and disgust with what has become of the American education system drives me to this. Let me just say I have always been deadly serious about the importance of excellent educational opportunities for all, and have maintained an almost Puritanical zeal for it, in spite of my occasionally jokester-like demeanors. But politicians are re-working the system into something resembling a business model enterprise, and the ill-educated American public who are the victims of this long ongoing shift in policy, procedures, and even common sense pedagogies, sit back and do nothing of substance to turn the tide. Nowadays if you are a student, a student of anything, you are perceived primarily as a customer of the schools, especially colleges. Teachers and staff are clerks. And that is wrong and perverse. A mind and heart in search of enrichment are not the same as a person in the vitamin aisle of Walgreens shopping for an energy booster. Today too many people entrusted with overseeing the operation of so many aspects of the education system, from administrators to members of schools' governing and advising boards, are ignorant of what makes up the successful and vibrant education culture. A large number of them have never taught in the classroom. Many such appointees do not even have college educations. Yet they are expected to pass wise judgment on issues of school operations both in and out of the classrooms, and on the delicate conditions of employment, such as salaries and benefits, that soundly impact the lives of an institution's often already underpaid employees. Too often those decisions lean in the direction of reduced benefits, no salary increases, larger class sizes, poorly equipped facilities, and generally large scale cuts in anything that can be cut. In short, those behind such reductive strategies are usually ignorant of what makes education work, and are not interested in getting to the bottom of it. And since such pariah are too often appointed and protected by the political system, the only solution to correcting the injustices is permanent elimination of them. Extermination. It's what any sane person will do when cockroaches overrun the house. It is Machiavellian in a warped way, to the tenth power, but it's a good way to get your attention. Actually, for the twenty-first century, Machiavelli is a bit of a pussy anyway. Indeed I will be thought of as another deranged evildoer in this growingly godless world, one devoid of true faith. To that however, I can only laugh out loud; for your goddamn gods and their delusional minions have directly or otherwise slain legions upon legions more than I ever would see fit, and for much less credible causes. Try to get something right this time people, or just go fuck yourselves

Hmmm. Not so bad for a first draft I guess, McDuff tells himself. It strays a bit toward the end. That last sentence won't make the cut in most places.

Actually, this is pretty bad stuff, he admits, glass of fresh squeezed orange juice now in hand. But what isn't pretty bad anymore anyway? He saves the thoughts as MiniManifesto.docx. and shuts down the computer.

A brazen black vulture alights in the top of the tall live oak just thirty feet to the right of the deck. Sean smiles up at the huge bird. That bird knows something, Mac suspects of the ominous scavenger. He gazes and muses ... now there's a more appropriate choice for Florida's state bird, better than that flakey mockingbird. The vulture oozes a dreadful awe that is the essence of this place, Florida, what Wallace Stevens refers to as venereal soil ... indeed a yingy-yangy wetlands ... maybe that's something of what Homer Simpson means when he calls it America's wang.

At two o'clock on the subtropical dot Martin Derrida pulls the smallish red van into McDuff's driveway. He is followed by a black Lexus sedan with darkly tinted windows, the driver thus hardly discernible. Sean is standing on the front porch smiling. As Martin gets out of the vehicle the professor, in gray t-shirt, tan shorts and Nikes, strolls out to meet him. They shake hands and both grin widely now.

"Good afternoon, McDuff. How are you feeling?" Martin's attire is a bit more formal—khakis, and dark blue dress shirt, sleeves rolled to the elbows.

The gist of Derrida's inquiry again eludes the good doctor. "Well, good, thank you lieutenant. How about yourself?'

"Likewise. But more specifically ... any pain, discomfort yet? Any symptoms of decline? You still look pretty damn good." He steps back to scrutinize McDuff's physique further, frowns slightly, then grins again. "You don't seem to have lost any weight. No skin discoloration, it appears from here. If I may be blunt, how's your shit looking? Are you eating right, able to keep your food down?"

A little put off by the detailed questioning at first, Sean frowns for a second, then shakes his head. "You know, Martin. I'm a little surprised at how, well, normal I still feel. I'm not on any strong meds yet. 'Have some headaches and chest pains off and on, but I think I can attribute that to plain old stress, and being, well, terminally pissed off."

The lieutenant looks pensive now. He nods. "Well McDuff, it may be that it's slowed down a little, even a lot, and you have a little more time than they predicted. Whether that's good or bad, only you can judge. When is your next checkup?"

"I've been ignoring the doctors. Their calls. Although I'm surprised that I haven't heard from the clinic now in about a month."

Derrida is quiet for about ten seconds, in thought, then says, "Have it your way. But let's get down to business here about your new car." He smiles and leads Sean to the vehicle's tailgate, opens it with the key remote, then lifts the lid of the carpeted floor storage niche behind the back bucket seats. Martin then removes an apparently false bottom of the cargo area to reveal a half-dozen cinder blocksize, smooth yellowish bricks, linked to each other with a series of heavy white wires.

"This," he declares with a broad smile, "is the heart and soul of our girl here. Meet Polly ... Polly Apocalypse. We like to give all of our special vehicles special names."

A quizzical frown appears on Sean's face now, but an approving one, and he is suddenly in the throes of an odd excitement. Derrida is still smiling at him. Then he slowly covers the bricks with the fake floor, closes the compartment, and shuts the tailgate, slamming it hard. McDuff is startled for an instant, and Martin notices.

"Don't worry. You cannot detonate this stuff that easily, even by dropping it from a skyscraper. It takes special high voltage charges, and that's part of what makes it so special, given its phenomenal destructive power."

Relief floods Sean, and he recovers his breath and asks, "Is that that high tech plastic stuff, you know, C4?"

"Close, but no cigar," Derrida replies. He motions the professor to the shaded porch. They walk there and up to the small glass-top table, and sit in the brown whicker chairs facing each other. The lieutenant removes a legal size envelope from his shirt pocket and places it on the table. His demeanor turns very serious now.

"Sergeant," he begins, then pauses. "Sergeant, what we have here is a top secret explosive agent, classified material, so far. But who knows how long that will last because the military has been using it, somewhat sparingly, in the Middle East now, in Afghanistan, in a few covert missions I am told. I know that it figured in a Plan B to take out bin Laden. But our beleaguered Prez got it right the first time. He's a better man than many give him credit."

Derrida glances off to his left at the clay flying eagle sculpture dangling from the porch overhang. He blinks. Then looks at McDuff and goes on, "The explosive is called A40, a hybrid form of plastic compounds. Pound for pound it is eight to ten times more powerful than the popular C4. You have enough there in Polly to obliterate a five story building on a half-acre foundation." He taps his index finger on the table six times, then goes on. "This stuff is being refined by our military to become the next truly formidable weapon of mass destruction, one that will match the effectiveness of atomic warheads, without the heavy polluting side effects. No radioactivity."

It takes a strong conscious effort by McDuff to prevent his jaw from dropping open in disbelief. Uneasiness creeps up his spine. Martin continues, sensing his customer's apprehension now. "Listen. As I said, you don't have to worry about accidentally setting it off. It would take a direct hit by a hell of a bolt of lightning to do that. So let me just go over the basics of what you need to know."

Sean nods and says, "Yes lieutenant. Give me the basics."

"OK. Under the front driver's seat is mounted a module about the size of an old cigar box. The wiring from the blocks is attached to it, and on the outside panel is a small on/off switch. That simply activates the power pack that will ignite the payload. It is more or less a receiver. To set it off you must use this detonator." From his front right pants pocket Derrida pulls a cylindrical object that is about the size of a hot dog, but black and somewhat flexible. He lays it on the table, then gets another object about the size of a double A battery out of his other pants pocket.

"This is the detonator," he says of the hot dog. "We call it 'the worm.' The red button is its top. It has a safety switch on the side here, under this tiny slide panel." He slides the cover open on the safety switch to show Sean. "Down is off, and up is on. The battery here goes in at the bottom, just like a flashlight. Do not install the battery until you are ready to use the device. In other words, until you are ready to set off the bomb. This special battery is temperamental, and only has a six-month shelf life."

McDuff nods and grins again. "Simple enough," he says. "So I don't need to plug it into the box under the seat or anything?"

"That's part of the beauty of it, sergeant. It's a remote, a transmitter, and a very powerful and sophisticated one." A broad smile now comes over Martin's face. "If you change your mind about going down with the ship, you can trigger the explosion from up to 800 meters away. You yourself, should take care to be at least 300 meters from ground zero when you do so, to avoid injury. And don't be watching, i.e. avoid eye contact. Also, keep low. The initial shock wave from an A40 blast travels in excess of ten thousand meters per second, and just as quickly the air roars back to fill the instantaneous void created by the explosion. One second the target is there, and a second later in a deafening and blinding flash, it's gone, vaporized. Imagine it's something like a quick category cazillion hurricane, a very very hot one." The lieutenant pauses and glares at the eagle again, then adds, "Depending on the base of the target, and the surrounding ground, you can get a crater six to sixteen meters deep and over fifty meters across."

Doctor McDuff breaks into a grimace of pleasure now. This is just amazing, he tells himself, so pleasantly monstrous. I'm happy to be almost dead, and have a way to break even. "Marvelous, Martin," he says. "Can I check out the interior while you're here, in case there's something I missed?"

"Please do McDuff."

They walk to the driveway. Derrida hands Sean the keys, and he opens the driver's side door of the van, squats down to examine the module under the seat. It is just as the lieutenant described it. He scrutinizes the dashboard, strokes the leather upholstery, and breathes in the new car smell. "Very nice vehicle," he tells Martin. "Very nice." After a minute or so of climbing in and out of the vehicle, bouncing in the plush seats front and back, admiring the dials and buttons, McDuff adds, "Excellent lieutenant. Excellent."

"Thank you, McDuff. Now let me brief you on a couple of other semi legal things, to put down any anxieties you may have, or that could arise, leading up to the big day, or perhaps afterwards."

"Well shoot," a puzzled Sean replies. Legal things?

"In the envelope on your table there are fake registration and insurance cards, in accordance with Florida law ... and also a bogus driver's license with your picture, lifted from your college's web site. It's not your name of course, and the address is a Naples location. My technical staff has hacked into the motor vehicles database and created a false record there, made a fake plate too of course, so even if you are stopped by the highway patrol, much less the local yokels, your records will come up legitimate. Just remember your alias information. It is very unlikely that you will be pulled over, but we take all precautions to ensure smooth sailing to your destination."

Sean's eyebrows rise. He once more smiles widely. "My good-ness, lieutenant. You people are terribly thorough. That's brilliant."

Martin Derrida laughs, then goes on, "So, to go back to the per-haps unlikely scenario that you decide against a pure suicide mission, rest assured that unless you are so careless as to allow someone to see you driving Polly, there is no chance you can be traced to the culprit device because every inch of the van will be vaporized by the explo-sion. I recommend that you leave the bogus paperwork in the car, so all scraps of incriminating evidence are destroyed." He pauses and scrutinizes McDuff again, as if to assure himself that Sean is digest-ing all of this, then adds, "Oh, and there's one of those handicap per-mits in the envelope too, the kind that hangs on the rearview mirror, in case your final plan requires a good parking spot."

An easy, peaceful feeling rolls over Sean M. McDuff now, a fore-seeable closure on this dirty trick of an existence that has stabbed him through and through. Indeed, it's a warm feeling at last. All that remains is to fine-tune the offensive. Nothing can stop him now but Sean Millington McDuff himself. Derrida sees the calm satisfaction that is taking over his old and fond acquaintance from the distant weekend warrior years, Doctor Sean McDuff. He reaches out his hand to grasp the professor's one more time. They clasp, then Mar-tin adds his other hand and firmly, enthusiastically applies a stron-ger beat, as if to ward off some inappropriate emotion. One of those bright afterthought grins takes hold of his rugged face and he says, "McDuff, I want you to know that if by some outrageous stroke of luck you get through this ... I mean that you don't take your own life, and your health does a turnaround ... well, I have a spot for you in our think tank. And it pays a lot more than your so-called teaching profession. That blows dead bears."

Sean is not sure how to respond. *That blows dead bears*, a Cana-dianism that he heard once in northern Washington, takes him back for a second to a tree-spiking gig where one of his cohorts smashed and bloodied a finger. But more importantly and immediately, he has just been offered a job by what is essentially a terrorist organization, or at least an elite support group. Is this not a beautiful example of life turning full circle twice, the perfect paradox, or what?

But he must answer. "Thank you very much, lieutenant. I'm flattered ... really. That's all I can say right now."

Derrida is oddly moved, and slightly saddened. Then he laughs, a laugh that comes quickly out of nowhere and jolts McDuff. "Oh hell. I nearly forgot. I would hate myself if I had left without saying this."

He stares up at the clean blue sky for a few seconds, then looks Sean in the eyes.

"I remember from Reserves how you were fond to quote Shakespeare under the damnedest conditions. You even got me interested." He puts his right hand on McDuff's left shoulder and says, "I wish you joy of the worm."

Then he turns and walks over to the waiting Lexus, and opens the passenger door.

Sean grins widely and shouts, "The worm is not to be trusted but in the keeping of wise people!" He raises his arm and pumps his fist. "Ha! Ha! Ha! Thank you again Martin!"

Derrida nods, gets in and shuts the door. The car backs out of the driveway, turns, and slowly disappears, crackling down the winding entry road. Could have sworn his eyes were watering there, McDuff tells himself. He chuckles. Fuckin' *Antony and Cleopatra* ... another zinger I didn't see coming.

Sean walks over to Polly and gets in. Better put this gal in the garage, he tells himself, in Sarah's old spot.

7
Reptilian Rhapsody

Morris Christian Bodey, appointed last year by the governor as the chairman for the Board of Trustees of Cypress State College, is one of the wealthiest men in southwest Florida, and a personal friend of the state's head honcho. It's a friendship purchased through campaign contributions and a deal on a new house. Bodey is owner, president, CEO, and informal Archdeacon of M.C. Bodey Enterprises, one of the largest real estate development corporations and homebuilders in the state. His grandfather, the legendary evangelist Corinthians Leviticus Bodey, otherwise fearfully known as Levi, preached hell-fire and brimstone to much of the southeastern United States for nearly forty years, until the unfortunate snake accident. God's antivenin works just fine with copperheads, but when CLB graduates to the formidable eastern diamondback rattlesnake for more effect, believers, and offerings ... well, it is said that his face was unrecognizable at the time of his departure for heaven. MC's father, Melvin, a man of the cloth as well, was regional clothing departments manager for Sears.

As Sean McDuff strolls the halls of the faculty office building on the Monday following Polly's arrival, talk of Bodey and the board's latest antics, and the upcoming meeting, fills the Humanities Division corridor.

"They've rescheduled it for March 17, the first Saturday of spring break, at eight a.m., no doubt an attempt to reduce the number of faculty who might make up an audience. Promotions are on the agenda, and something about continuing salary freezes. And there are rumors that even those who are promoted, if approved, may not get the bump in pay because of hard times, as they call it." John Collins, of the history department, shakes his head in disgust and just walks away from his gathered colleagues from the social sciences, almost as if he is leaving it up to them to do something about it.

Sean continues the few steps more to his office. Typical, he says to himself. All bitch and no bite. He walks past the reception station of administrative assistant Carla Ramirez, home sick today, and ducks into his inner sanctum and closes the door.

Oh, let's see here, McDuff thinks, as he sits down, opens a top desk drawer and removes his academic calendar for spring 2012. Hmmm. Oh, so the board meeting was originally scheduled for the twenty-ninth, a Wednesday evening. Oh Bodey, Bodey, Bodey, you snake you. I give you credits toward your Conniver Honor Badge. For indeed a meeting during spring break, and on a weekend morning, will definitely keep the sheep from the door. No doubt you have mass fucking up your dirty sleeves. Well, Mister Chairman, you are in for a surprise that can only be measured in megatons. My girlfriend Polly and I shall pay you and yours a visit on that fateful morning.

A knock at the door stops McDuff's soliloquy.

"Enter," he says loudly. Barry Hope opens the door and smiles.

"Professor Hope!" McDuff is pleased to see him. They have not socialized yet this term, so some catch up is in order. "Please have a seat, Barry." Sean points to the chair opposite his, then says, "you can leave the door open."

"Thank you, Doctor," as Barry sits down. "And how are you on this merry Monday? Sorry to tamper with your reclusivity."

"It's OK. I was just trying to keep out the chatter for a few minutes. I'm fine. How about you?"

Hope places his hands on his knees for a second, looks down, then up, and smiles shyly at McDuff. "I just want to thank you for the kind words on my evaluation, and in my application for promotion."

Sean waves his right hand sideways, shakes his head **no** and says, "I should be thanking you, Barry. You're an excellent instructor, a credit to the college community. You are a credit to the department in every way, and your taste in beer is above average." He wonders if he's gushing, going overboard with the praise, and tempers his sincerity with, "You know me well enough too, fella, to realize I am not dealing you bullshit here."

Barry Hope laughs, and seems to relax a bit more. "Well thank you again anyway. I guess now all that's left is for me to await the college's decision on my promotion?"

"Not exactly," McDuff replies grinning. "Myself, the committee chair, Dean and President have signed the papers. It's a done deal that just needs the rubber stamp of the board of trustees. Your next contract will reflect your move up to Assistant Professor. So congratulations."

"But I thought that the board had final say."

"There are a few misinformed people around here that think that, but they are wrong. Once you are approved officially by the college as you have been, case closed. It's state law. So technically what the board gets next month is not a recommendation, but something that merely needs their signature of acknowledgement." Sean considers telling Barry about his annoying chat with the clueless EP back in December, but then decides not. No point in causing him anxiety. Let the EP try to screw things up, and make an even bigger jackass stable out of the board meeting.

"So Barry, if you are not informed of the college's decision by the end of the semester, contact James Huggins over in Naples. He's an attorney with a lot of experience in education cases. And he's reasonable. He'll know exactly what to do." Huggins was the lawyer who encouraged Mac to sue the college over his forced sabbatical following Sarah's death.

Hope frowns and blinks several times. "Do you think it will come to that, really?"

"No, no it shouldn't. Clarise Robbins, an older board member who was not appointed by our distinguished governor, is an attorney who knows the ropes. If she is present I'm sure she will straighten them out." Too bad if she is, though, McDuff realizes. Then another unpleasant possibility enters his thoughts. "You don't ... ." His throat clogs briefly and a rush of pain shoots up the right side of his head. "I mean, are you planning on attending the meeting ... to be in the audience, even though the audience is not allowed to verbally participate?" He struggles to hide his uneasiness now. Barry Hope seems not to notice his boss's slight panic.

"Oh hell no," he says quickly. "Are you ready for this?"

Sean is ready for anything that affirms a negative reply as to Mr. Hope's attendance. Barry nods his head playfully and says, "Hope Rollins invited me to go to Key West with her for the St. Patrick's Day Bar Stroll. Her aunt and uncle have a big condo there that we can use, since they'll be out of town."

This surprises Sean in a good way. He grins and asks, "Are you dating now? I mean, I'm not prying, but Hope is a fine instructor as well, and an interesting young woman with a good sense of humor."

"We did a happy hour a couple of Fridays ago, the one you can-celled on after postponing the department meeting. We hit it off OK I guess. I'm not sure I'd call this trip a date, or that she sees it like that either. She did emphasize that the condo has three bedrooms. I think maybe her girlfriend in Miami had to cancel, so I'm her second choice. But I don't mind."

Barry looks down at his shoes for a second, puts his elbows on his knees for a moment and his head between his hands, as if recover-ing from mild exhaustion. Then he sits up straight, looks at McDuff and turns serious. "Have you been feeling alright lately Mac? You've been hard to find. And Carla says you've taken a few sick days."

McDuff hesitates. Be careful here, he tells himself. I have been aloof, removed. But I don't want to let Barry in on anything, even though he's the closest thing to a friend I have here. He's a good guy. His concern is genuine. Think quick.

"Thanks for asking Barry. Actually I've had some bouts with migraines lately, nothing terribly serious, and I have them on the run now. The doc says it's mostly, or probably, stress related. The old head has a tendency to come a little unscrewed too when you approach the half-century mark I guess."

"Oh ... oh hell, I'm sorry Mac." Hope seems to breathe in some relief at the news. "Well, I guess this place doesn't help sometimes either, what with all the political turmoil coming down from Talla-hassee." He nods and laughs softly, "Right?"

Now Sean is laughing. "Truer words, etcetera, etcetera, Barry."

The instructor glances at his wristwatch and says, "OK, that's a relief. But now it seems I have a composition class calling." He gets up out of his chair and walks to the door, turns back and says, "Thanks again, Mac. And if the headaches return, don't be shy about calling me if I can help with anything. You know, like covering your classes or something, all right?"

"Thank you very much, Barry. I'll keep that in mind." He glances down at his desk, then back at Barry. "Give your writers hell today," he grins. Hope nods and disappears out the door.

8
Valentine's Day

On February 14 Sean dismisses his eleven a.m. composition class early and goes back to his office just before noon. At the beginning of class that day he finds a handmade card on the podium speckled with hearts and palm trees, wishing him a Happy Valentine's Day, signed by all fifteen class members. He smiles and tells them he is cancelling the planned quiz, and they applaud, give a few high-fives, then settle in and listen with interest to his bit on inflated diction, which mostly involves him reading passages of especially awful and wordy renditions of clear and simple prose. "Call me Ishmael," for example, is inflated to read, "Let it be known by you and others of the world that the preferred nomenclature for myself is indubitably Ishmael." Since the supposed lesson comes off as something like a stand-up comic's routine, the class leaves happy, and early, for lunch.

McDuff now looks out his office window at the three-story administration building a hundred yards across the quadrangle from him. It is the newest and ugliest building on campus, situated on numerous sixteen-foot load-bearing beams of steel and concrete, which gives it a whopping four story appearance. The open area under the first floor is reserved parking for those who work there: two dozen various administrators, including the President; Records and Registration staff; and a few academic advisors. Shortly after it's opening three years ago McDuff dubs it The Tower of Babble, and the name spreads to the student body vernacular as well. The TB is home to a sprawling executive board room on the first floor, which overlooks athletic fields that extend a few hundred yards to stands of palmetto and various trees that make up a green buffer between the campus proper and the river and wetlands that flow north to south along the eastern edges of Cypress State College. A small walking path winds about fifty yards through the thick green to a small wood observation deck near the river's western shore. The deck has a winding staircase to its top, nearly forty feet above the ground. It is sparingly used by college biology and environmental science classes. McDuff and Sarah used to take their binoculars there in the spring and observe the rookeries of wood storks and egrets up and down the stream, the nesting birds a bright white accent to the ambivalent, marvelous greenness of the wetlands.

His recollection is interrupted by a light tapping on the doorframe to his office.

"Hi Doctor McDuff!"

He turns to see Jane Green standing there, smiling, holding books, notebooks, and a file folder in her arms. His approaching melancholy falls off and he greets her enthusiastically. "Well hello there, Jane! How's the semester going so far?" He moves to his chair behind the desk, points and says "Please sit down, if you have time."

"Oh thank you sir. My classes are done for today. I have those names and addresses for you that we talked about last month."

"Yes. Yes. The letters of reference, of course. Hand them over."

She hands him the file folder and says, "And yes, the classes are going very well so far."

"I'm not surprised, ma'am." He opens the folder, flips through the three or four sheets of paper and says, " Hmmm, Gulf Coast and Atlantic, I see. Good choices, from what I know of their respective programs."

"I hope so. But I've got my fingers crossed." She glances out the window, then smiles nervously at Sean again. He senses she needs encouragement, some good words and body language. Out of seemingly nowhere he is able to conjure it.

"I know a few people at both institutions, and will let them know I do ... tactfully, of course. So your biggest problem will be choosing between the two, come summer. Take the one that is going to offer the most money, and a nice car."

She blushes and laughs. "I'll remember your sound advice, sir, even though I don't intend to play basketball or volleyball at either place."

McDuff flips through the folder again and feigns intense scrutiny, then frowns and says, " Oh, I see ... yes ... you're one of those greenies." Then he puts his right index finger on the top of one of the pages, raises his eyebrows, "Aah of course, it says so right here," tapping his finger on the page, "Green, Jane Green." Shit, I hope she knows I'm just trying to lighten her mood, he tells himself. I'm getting carried away.

When he looks up at Jane she is throbbing hysterically and trying to hold back the laughs. Sean is relieved. He smiles once more and says, "Seriously, Jane, I'm sure you are a shoo-in. So just kick back and finish your business here. You'll be fine. I'll get the references out this week, OK?"

Now she is wiping small tears from her eyes, but they are not, McDuff intuits, exactly tears of laughter. He suddenly feels foolish and dumbfounded, helpless a little, and desperate to restore her.

"Jane? I didn't mean to come off so flippantly. I'm very serious about wanting to help you ... I'm sorry if I ... I mean ...."

"No. No. It's OK." She wipes her cheeks with her hand and smiles, then forces a laugh. "I'm sorry. I'm really sorry." She starts to get up to leave and Sean gets out of his chair and walks over to her.

"Don't leave," he says, putting a hand on her shoulder. "Please sit ... tell me if you want to, or need to. What's going on? You've had a bad week, maybe, right? Imagine we're at Poopdecks, without the beer."

God, I hope that works, he tells himself.

Jane smiles and her face gains composure again. "I'm really sorry," she says.

McDuff gently closes the office door, then sits down on the front of the desk and looks at her. He smiles. She starts to explain. Sits back down.

"Things just got a little out of control these last few days. I have two papers due, and I haven't gotten enough sleep because mom is in the hospital with pneumonia, and, well, I'm just exhausted, and worried, and ... well."

"Oh hell, Jane. I'm sorry to hear about your mother. Is there anything I can do to help you?" What the fuck did I say that for, Sean barks to himself. I'm no good to anyone anymore. Get real McDuff!

"Is your mom going to be all right?"

Jane Green sits up straight, her composure reclaimed, and she smiles as if the tears and broken syllables never happened. Sean is shocked by her quick recovery. She's damn resilient, he thinks, a very strong young woman. Reminds me a little of Sarah, a very tall Sarah.

"Oh, Doctor McDuff. Yes, mom will be OK, probably in a few days. Thank you for asking, and understanding," she says as she stands up quickly. "I'm so embarrassed. You don't have to write those letters for me. I'll understand."

He feels close to human for the first time in months, and calmly says, "Jane. Jane, I want to write them, now more than ever. And it's not a matter of feeling sorry. Not at all. I want to help a really good student, and more importantly a fine person, in any way I can. And don't you ever suppose otherwise ... or I'll never buy you another beer." He smiles, but then thinks, I hope she doesn't take that as sneaky way of suggesting we go on a date. Holy crap, what the hell is wrong with me, besides the liver?"

Jane takes a step toward the door. "Thank you again," she repeats.

McDuff gets up from the desk and crosses her path to open the door. They gently collide and her long hair brushes his cheek.

She stops, and says, "Oh, I can get it."

He doesn't reply, and just grasps the doorknob, turns it slowly, and opens the door. The administrative assistant is seated at her desk outside and looks over and smiles. McDuff steps back to give Jane clear passage.

"Really good to see you again, Ms. Green. Check back with me when you can on all this."

Jane's grin broadens, and she replies, "I will Doctor McDuff. Thanks a million again." She glides calmly out into the hall and disappears.

McDuff walks back to his desk chair and plops down, breathes deeply and sighs. He turns to look out the window again at the Tower of Babble. His rush fades fast. He looks at Jane's folder and starts to think about the letters he will write. I just hope, he quips to himself, that she gets accepted before the college realizes she has references from a murdering nutcase.

"Alas, no hug today," he mutters.

9
The Vulture Dialogues

That vulture, the one appearing in the oak tree off Mac's deck in early February, begins to make habit of lighting there regularly around dinnertime now. Thus on the last Sunday in February begin the vulture dialogues, which run sporadically into the stricken ides of March, where McDuff's fatal destiny hovers and glows like wormy larvae in the caves of so many horror stories. Poe's "The Raven" is a shimmering analogy many might attach to part of this: there is the grieving, shattered man whose love has been snatched by heinous Fate; and of course we have the dark bird of omen, mystery, and unhinging, redundant lines. But the pinch of newt in this witches broth is Sean himself, being eaten alive from the inside by malignancy and souring emotion. It is rot and stench of multiple dimensions.

Sean names the black vulture Victor. He speaks at Victor. He imagines Victor's replies, or rather he translates the very occasional grunts and hisses that gurgle up from the great bird's throat. The damaged professor, then, is a thing somewhere between the schizophrenic Gollum of *The Lord of the Rings* films (debating the fate of The Precious with his evil side) and that castaway Tom Hanks character, who talks to a volleyball.

"Good evening, Victor. And what have you been doing to celebrate the Sabbath today." McDuff, seated at the teak deck table, opens a bottle of draught Guinness, takes a sip. "Ah. Can I offer you a brew?"

Victor blinks **no**.

"Hmmm," he continues. "Had a rough happy hour, did we? I don't blame you then." Sean goes on to explain to Victor that he is dying and, according to predictions, soon. That he misses his wife still, and it is too often unendurable. Then there's The Profession. He has come to loathe the influence of business politics on it all, and feels sorry for his students. He still likes enough of them to keep doing a good job, to give them their money's worth, although he would never say *money's worth* publicly because the phrase has too much of a retailer-world ring to it. His somewhat forced enthusiasm wards off suspicion that he is on The Edge, on the brink of a terrible statement that will rock ivory towers, coffeehouses, and open mics across the country. The globe.

Victor seems to know this. But he does not give a shit, or even a flying shit, being a large bird. He just sits, perches actually, and dreams of roadkill, and the gang. That feral pig struck down by the redneck driving the Ram was a hell of a party.

"Well I'll tell you what I did, to honor Mother Earth," Sean raises his voice. "I finalized my last will and testament, and will send it off to my attorney some fine day soon. I'm leaving it all to Everglades National Park. No joke. Almost wish I could be around to see how they're going to figure that one out."

"Cheers." He tips the bottle up at the big bird.

———————

A week later, after a dinner of black beans and brown rice, and contraband snook, McDuff is reclined in a lounge chair by the deck rail with a snifter of his all time favorite rum, the no longer available Guatemalan Zaya. Victor lands on his oak perch again, emits a guttural hiss, and appears to urinate on his own legs. It's an unseasonably warm evening, so urohydrosis—as Sean recalls the name of this disgusting habit—is an exercise some animals use to cool off their limbs and lower extremities. Some seals do it, but not in the Disney animations.

"Gross Victor!" Sean scolds. "But a really cheap alternative to air conditioning. I suspect that one of my school's vice presidents will sometimes do that rather than get up out of the chair and lower the thermostat. His office smells like it." McDuff drinks of the bottle of beer and sings, "Oh metaphors, metaphors, metaphors!" Then he savors a sip of the rum. Yes, he has the chaser sequence backwards, but that's life now. Reverse gusto. He gets up out of the chair and begins to pace, think, resolve. Lights in his head flicker. Coincidentally, and perpetuating the pun of nature, a solitary flicker alights on the trunk of Victor's oak, and begins to dance and peck.

"Victor," McDuff says softly but urgently. "You must fly to Tallahassee in the morning, on the first vapors. Show the leaders your solution. Pissing on yourself," and he begins to laugh like a villain. "Oh yes! An efficient and cost effective way to relieve one of the premier side effects of climate change. If the leaders can train the poor and the middle classes in this energy saving method ... to eschew air conditioning ...my god the money it will save them ... and the electric power that can be stored for the whimsy of the wealthy. My god, Victor! I am verily astounded that the Republicans have not made it part of their economic recovery plan ... yet."

The professor takes another sip of Zaya, then a swallow of the Guinness. He has it right now. He feels a sense of sense creeping, perhaps, into American government once more, and maybe the education system. Smiling he conjects, "Why, CSC can be the first state school to offer a course. **Urohydrosis 101:** An introduction to the health and comfort benefits of pissing yourself. Three credit hours. No text required. A requirement for all baccalaureate programs."

———

On Friday, March 16, the last day of classes before spring break, McDuff cancels, phoning Ms. Ramirez at eight a.m. to tell her his migraine is back and he has an appointment. It is of course fabrication. He is in grave and serious preparatory mode now. "Feel better, sir," Carla says as Sean is hanging up.

After a bowl of grape nuts and blueberries, in 2% milk, he contemplates his wardrobe for tomorrow. It will not be the shorts and CSC tank top he is presently wearing. Few men approaching the half century mark on Earth can wear such attire, morning or otherwise, without looking a little silly. McDuff is fit, slim, almost zero body fat, with only a sprinkling of gray hairs in his still thick scalp. A tad over six feet tall, he still looks twenty years younger despite his plummeting health within, and lava between his ears.

On the big bedroom chair he lays out his favorite Lee jeans, a long-sleeve dark green t-shirt, his old Tilley hat (a small brimmed sailing hat from the days he and Sarah used to weekend up in Fort Myers and charter that old Morgan Out Islander). Hiking boots, heavy white socks, and his tan fishing vest spotted with pockets of various size and depth complete the outfit.

He has a banana and orange juice for lunch, saving himself for the planned last supper of baked chicken breast, steamed asparagus, and mashed potatoes with gravy.

Mac's mood is quietly melancholy, but a strong determination for closure gives him an unusual focus and calm while he completes various bits of house and yard chores, as if it's just another day in the life of a lonely widower. To his satisfaction, one bottle of Drano unclogs the bathroom sink. Just three eight-inch pieces of end branches need trimmed from the Trinidad lime tree, to get rid of the leaf miners.

After dinner McDuff goes out to the deck and reclines in the lounge chair once more, a bottle of stout and a snifter of Zaya in hands. It is a healthy three-ounce portion, and fittingly all that is left of the last bottle. Pretty fuckin' sad, he thinks, but too too fitting.

The March sun is about a half hour from setting. Victor, dark, formidable, and strangely noble, tops the live oak again. Sean looks up and smiles. "Vic my man," he says, "sleep in tomorrow, and stay away from campus. There won't be enough pieces of dead meat anyway to make it worth your while. My sources assure me. Unless the explosion triggers cardiac arrest in anyone close by. But even then your chances for a good meal are slim, my friend." The vulture hisses softly as McDuff grins. His imagination skips to the future he will not see, and conjures headlines and leads ... journalism he once called it ... reporting ... Ha!

Powerful Explosion Levels College Building, Killing at Least Fifty

Terrorism Suspected in CSC Bombing

FBI Takes Over in CSC Bombing Investigation

Still No Clues to Explosion That Killed Board of Trustees, Several College Administrators and Employees During Spring Break

Profilers Suspect College Bomber Was a Sick Loser of Unfathomable and Pathetic Dimensions, Probably Sparsely Educated

Whataya mean 'sparsely educated,' McDuff thinks. Hmmm, all the more urgent that I get my MiniManifesto into the proper hands. I'll email a copy to Barry, and a few south Florida newspapers ... from my laptop in the morning, before I punch the worm. There's WiFi all over the tower. I'll open the car windows and blare some Black Sabbath. How dramatic is that? Oh damn ... I never got around to revising the manifesto, but whataya gonna do?

"Oh will this ever be something to see. Will it ever, huh, Victor?"

"But ... hell ... I'm not going to see it."

A sharp pain begins under Sean's breastbone and seems to trickle down to his stomach. He tries to belch, but cannot, and gets up out of the chair clutching himself. He staggers to the kitchen and takes out the bottle of famotidine pills in the closet over the sink ... fills a glass with water and takes two tablets, then sits down on the floor and waits for relief. Five minutes. Ten minutes. It begins to subside.

That is the worst one yet, he tells himself. I'm going down fast I think.

He gets to his feet and walks back out to the lounge chair, sits, sips the beer. Victor pushes out of the tree and flaps his wings, tiny grunting, and heads out for wherever his nightly perch must be.

Sean McDuff's eyes water and he shouts, stuttering, "See ya buddy ... thanks for listening!"

Then ... a small horror creeps up on his raison d'être. On the possible other hand, Mac frowns, I'm going to be seen as a reclusive mad man who had everyone fooled. Given the attitudes of the enemy, the politicians, toward teachers today ... shit! I'll just be giving them more ammunition to inflict their goddamn business model Fascist feudal system changes throughout: regular psychological testing for teachers; yearly job evaluations based on criteria that have nothing to do with classroom reality; accountability based on teaching to The Test, and if you just happen to have a batch of sub par students one semester, and it shows ... it's your goddamn fault ... and time clocks ... fucking time clocks!

"Aaaah!"

He buries his head in his hands and shakes. Then he jumps up and walks to the rail overlooking the darkening riverscape.

"No! No!"

I can't be destroyed too, not yet. Exterminate the brutes. Yes. But I have to be around long enough to see how the lesson pans out, then maybe confess and explain and gripe and ... maybe not. What can they do to me? I'm not going to live long enough to even go to trial. When the dust and speculative shit settle, I can at least attempt to ... to ... suggest a dialogue or something. Suggest why or how someone could have done this, this terrible thing.

Oh fuck, confess nothing, he retracts. If Martin is right, there will be no way they can pin it on me, if I'm very careful, cunning.

McDuff strolls back inside to the refrigerator and gets another beer, then returns to the deck. A bright moon is rising. A new plan bubbles up from his festering soul.

I'll get there at least an hour before meeting time and park Polly in the handicap spot that is directly under the board room. Then cross the soccer fields to the hammock and make my way to the overlook. I'll take my best binoculars, so I can see the building very well from there. The big boardroom windows face the fields, and I'll probably even be able to see who's at the meeting, plus be far enough away to survive the blast. It won't be out of range for the worm.

As for getting back home ... hmmm. This house is only five miles straight up river, and it's not a tough walk. Hell, Sarah and I did it two or three times, a few years ago. We'd pack a lunch, take my car to campus. Walk out to the observation platform and bird watch. Then take in the hiking and crude game trails and all that, as we walked upstream, a few hours worth of mother nature. And when we got home we could take her car back down the winding state road and go back and pick up mine.

Sean takes a large swallow of stout now, and a deep breath.

Yes, he goes on to himself. I need to be around to, well, monitor the fallout, at least for a little while. And I have the Colt, if or when things get too bad.

10

Three, Two, One!

About a half hour before sunrise McDuff pulls Polly Apocalypse into the handicap parking spot that sits directly under the board room of the administration building, The Tower of Babble, where the spring meeting of the school's mistrusted board of trustees will commence shortly after eight. The campus is dark, except for a few security lamps here and there. Not surprisingly Sean sees no other vehicles on his short drive through campus, as school security on weekends is sparse. There are no orange cones in the parking spaces under the building, to save convenient spots for the board members. Given the rumors of no pay raises again, a move endorsed by the board, security becomes forgetful. Plus, it's spring break. Yes, spring break! Sean instructed his classes last week to be thankful of their geographical situation. That they do not have to get on the traditional college bandwagon and head off to Florida, because they are already here. A few smiled and nodded.

It takes him about ten minutes to cross the athletic fields and quadrangle, surely undetected, find the winding walking path through the hammock, and arrive at the tall platform that overlooks the river. He climbs the stairs to the topmost deck and settles in, raising his binoculars to focus the target. Sunrise blooms in the east. A few cars have pulled in under the building, where lights begin to illuminate the windows, including the boardroom now. Mac's only small fear is that some Audubon Society geeks will be along to conduct a morning watch of the rookeries. That will require his disappearing to the undergrowth, and just timing the blast by guesswork. But so far he is the solitary observer. He feels in his lower vest pocket for the worm. It is cool and ready. The battery is in his upper left pocket, velcroed shut until approaching lift-off. In the pockets of his brown cargo pants (he nixed the jeans option for comfort and more storage) is a bagged olive loaf sandwich, a banana, and a small bottle of Gatorade, for the long upstream trek home. He is also packing a hefty Swiss army knife. Tick. Tick.

McDuff focuses again on the wide boardroom windows and the gathering group, probably twenty strong by now. The EP is there waddling about like the nasty penguin he is. Sean can make out M.C. Bodey as well, and recognizes several more board members and college administrators. "The core scum are here," he mutters. But it's too bad that a skeleton crew of registrar people and counselors have to work the half-day today, due to the dubious business efficiency sought by the board.

The sun clears the tree line to the east, putting the campus in full morning glow. At eight fifteen it appears that all are seated now for the meeting. McDuff unhands the binoculars and lets them dangle from his neck. He takes the worm out of his vest, then removes the battery from the upper pocket.

Worm in his right hand, battery in the left one, he stares at them for a moment and takes a deep breath. Then he unscrews the bottom of the worm and inserts the battery, and screws the cap back on. Just like a flashlight, as Martin said. He slides open the little compartment on the side, where the detonator transmitter's safety switch sits. He flicks it up and on. The red trigger button on the top of the worm begins to glow. McDuff gently places the worm back in his vest pocket, then raises the binoculars to his eyes.

He scans the T of B one more time, noticing a tall woman in jeans and brownish jacket halfway up the steps and approaching the building's automatic double doors. Oh well, he says to himself, another innocent victim. In a cartoonish squeaky voice he remarks, "You knew the job was dangerous when you took it, Fred."

One more quick glance back to the window, then back to the woman !!!!!!! a terrible, frigid shock like arctic Novocain rockets through his body as he pulls the binoculars deeper into his eye sockets and !!!!!!!!!!!!!!!!!!!!!!!!!!!

"FUCK! OH FUCK, NO!"

He pushes the binoculars harder against his eye sockets as the building's doors slide open and the woman disappears into their dark maw.

"What the HELL is she doing here!!"

Jane Green.

Sean drops the binoculars, quickly turns, his entire being quaking, sits down hard on the floor of the observation deck. He starts to breathe heavily as his heart rate rises. He places his hands over his face ... and begins to wail and weep.

"Jesus Christ! Jesus H. Fucking Christ," he stammers and gasps. He lowers his hands palms up and stares at them now in bewilderment. Tears race down his cheeks, drip from his chin, and make faint tapings on his vest and pants like a weak drizzle in late subtropical winter.

Blinking at his hands, trying to clear his eyes, shaking his hands up and down he says, "These are not mine. What am I doing? Where? Where have I been?"

The weeping and throbbing slow, then stop, and his breathing and heartbeat begin a return to something close to normal.

McDuff stands up after a minute and turns to face the campus again. He carefully removes the worm from his pocket, flicks off the safety switch, then unscrews the bottom cap and takes out the battery, returning the perfect couple to their separate pockets once more.

"Holy fucking shit," he whispers, still breathing a bit heavily, "where have I fucking been?" He rubs his eyes, gasps for some more air, and thinks ... at least I don't have to walk home now.

But the rub is not gone. How do I get back to Polly and drive the hell out of here unseen? I especially cannot be seen by Jane.

McDuff climbs down out of the observation deck and takes the trail out of the hammock, to the edge of campus, easy to discern due to fresh mowings. He walks slowly along the perimeter of palmettos and small shrubs, occasionally stopping to look into the brush, or raising his binoculars and peering up at the trees. He is playing Audubonite. After about three hundred yards of trekking the edges of campus he turns to walk in to retrieve Polly, as he is now north of the Tower of Babble and less likely to be noticed. His hat, pulled down to meet the wrap-around sunglasses, hides his face well. And there is no one in sight, save for a security vehicle, a used golf cart, motoring away from the distant student union building to the west.

He reaches Polly. Gets in and starts the engine. In the rearview mirror now he sees Jane Green getting into her SUV. He waits for her to start it up and pull away. His heart races once more.

"This cannot be real," he says. "Where have I been?"

———

The rest of Sean McDuff's Attack Saturday is reserved. He shortens his traditional St. Patrick's Day beverage list of Guinness, Smithwick's, and Harp (one each), and limits the intake of Old Bushmill's ten years old single malt to three modest shots. Trembling for hours, he feels as if he's just returned from uncharted nightmare zones, and no idea as to how or why he was lucky enough to survive ... vague as to how he got here ... wounds that must heal, or else. He avoids looking into the mirrors in the house. During a brief walk along the river he won't gaze directly into the water, reluctant to see his reflection, reverse Narcissism. He nearly consummated a horror beyond articulation. Now McDuff prays he is on that pot-holed road out of Hades, but has little idea as to how many miles to go before he sleeps.

II
Dead Wrong

Sitting Sunday on the porch deck, while the sun sets behind him, he realizes that Victor has not returned for two days now, although yesterday Sean was asleep shortly after dark.

I need answers, he thinks. I'll call the clinic first thing tomorrow and try to get some follow up, some idea. Damn it. Still feel somewhat OK. The attacks and discomfort, nausea ... I think it's more acid reflux. The pills work. So really, how long do I have?

I want to know what happened at the board meeting. Maybe I'll call Mavis in a day or two.

'Wonder if Barry and Hope are back? Maybe we can have dinner this week.

I should try to call Nash. Maybe.

I'd like to know how Jane's mother is doing.

Then there's that most monstrous subtext of all ... what the hell is he going to do with Polly Apocalypse? She's like a Las Vegas bride, met there in a tacky casino, and married in a drunken stupor of cosmic and poorly comic proportion. Maybe worse.

"I can't leave that goddamn thing in my garage, or try to give it back to the lieutenant. Aye carumba!"

———

Nine o'clock Monday morning he calls the clinic and speaks with a Miss Money, who puts him on hold for about three minutes. When she returns she sounds very relieved and congenial.

"Mr. McDuff?"

"Yes." Since I couldn't get the Surgeon General to sit here and hold for me.

"I apologize for the long wait, sir. But I just spoke with Doctor Watson, he's our new chief of staff, and he wants to see you first thing in the morning for a consultation, and he wants to run a few more tests. Can you be here at eight?"

"Doctor Watson? But my consulting physician is Doctor Breadloaf."

"Oh, I'm sorry sir, but Doctor Breadloaf is no longer with us. I assure you that Doctor Watson is familiar with your case, and your condition. He very much wants to see you. He's a fine Doctor."

Sean sighs and wonders what new bad news awaits, or what revolutionary new treatment may be available for the right guinea pig with a full wallet. Curiosity, McDuff believes, does not always kill the cat, so he agrees to be there at eight.

After a morning of various image scans and blood work, a little before noon Sean McDuff is sitting in the office of Doctor Watson, he presumes, as he was led there by a young blonde haired woman in aqua scrubs, all smiles. The doctor is but seconds behind her, walks in quickly, grinning, and offers a professionalesque handshake which Sean rises to engage.

"Mister McDuff. I'm Matt Watson, and I am glad to finally meet you. Please have a seat."

Watson, rather than taking his chair behind the desk, leans his buttocks on the front of the desk and opens a thick folder containing negatives, images, all sorts of medical documents indecipherable to a mere Ph.D. in language and literature like Sean Millington McDuff. Flipping through them almost comically, Watson shakes his head, takes a deep breath, then plops the folder down beside him, a small, odd grin on his face now. Sean gives off a smile and is unable to speak. He wonders if the doctor is high, and what sort of dark lunacy is coming next.

McDuff breaks the short silence with, "OK Doctor, how long do I have now?"

"How long would you like?" the doctor replies.

"What?"

"Mr. McDuff, I'll be blunt with you, and begin by offering my sincere apologies on behalf of this institution."

Could I drop over dead any second now, Sean asks himself. What the hell is with this guy? He must have a sicker sense of humor than I. "What exactly are you saying," he finally asks.

"Sean," the doctor begins, "you don't mind if I call you *Sean*, do you?"

"Hell, you can call me Ishmael if you like." The doctor of philosophy grows impatient now.

"Sean ... there is nothing wrong with you. And I doubt that there ever was. You do not have a hepatocellular carcinoma, liver cancer, or anything fatal or dangerous."

"What?"

"You are a healthy, middle-aged man for the most part. Maybe a mild blood pressure issue, but otherwise ...." Watson raises his hands, palms open, in one of those what-the-heck informal gestures.

"What?"

"Your MRIs and other scans last summer were false positives, and the radiologist at the time should have detected that. The accompanying blood work was likewise inaccurate, or perhaps blown out of proportion by the attending physician, Doctor Breadloaf, who, by the way is no longer employed here. In fact, to be honest, he has left the state of Florida in the wake of some embarrassing legal issues, if you get the picture." Watson's face grows more serious now, as truth infects the room.

"What!!"

Doctor Watson rubs his brows and eyes with his right hand and then continues. "Around early December, when all of this began to surface, we tried calling you several times to get you to come in for a re-evaluation. I guess you weren't taking our calls. But whatever the case ... well, did you ever begin to suspect that something was wrong, I mean with Doctor Breadloaf's report, and his predictions as to how you might expect to feel as the supposed cancer spread? And by the way, please don't think I'm faulting you in any way, for not getting to the bottom of this in a more timely manner."

"What!"

McDuff is stunned in a way he cannot completely fathom, or express. Ambivalence to the highest degree rocks his being, and he thinks, do I kiss this man, or go back and get Polly and blow this place to smithereens? Take a cab home.

"What?" he says again.

"Sean," the doctor places his hands on his thighs and conjures an even more serious and somewhat sympathetic look. "I won't try to imagine the terrible anxieties you must have gone through over these past months, the depression, fear, and range of emotions that must be ripping your life apart ... and for no other reason but the carelessness and incompetence of two or three supposed professionals, who by the way are no longer employed here, as you may have already heard."

The professor is shocked and nearly speechless, worse than when he watched his father fall to his death from the Garry Creek Bridge.

"And I don't suppose there is anything of real worth that we can do to make up for it all. But this may surprise you, and I wish I could think of another way to say it, but, off the record, you are welcome to sue the clinic for any sort of damages your lawyer can come up with. Our legal team is expecting such, on at least two or three fronts, thanks to Doctor Breadloaf and his crackpot radiologist friend. And we are prepared to make healthy settlements." Watson gives a great sigh, glad to have gotten it all out. "I am really sorry, Mister McDuff. And I hope you'll just give this some thought once the shock wears off, and the outrage goes away."

McDuff is in the grips of a dumbfounded glow. Doctor Watson continues.

"The symptoms that brought you here were most likely caused by what you might call a kick-ass strain of heartburn, acid reflux syndrome. And goddamnit that's something the attending physician should have figured out early, instead of going off dialing for carcinoma. He already had results of your stress tests too. So any cardiovascular problems were off the table." The doctor shakes his head and continues, "Again, my apologies Mister McDuff. I see that you take famotidine, as needed, and that is most likely all you need right now. If it requires anything stronger I'll check you out and give you some other pills to try. Free."

A half-smile comes to Sean's face as he rubs his right temple. After the brief rubbing he shakes his head, exhales heavily, emits a short laugh. "What ... what the hell can I say? I ... I'm relieved and happy to know this, certainly. It's ... it's like I've been in a coma at the bottom of an outhouse. And I'm waking up, and glad to be crawling out. But it still stinks."

Doctor Watson holds back a chortle. He did not smell that analogy coming. That's a bizarre way to look at it, he tells himself. The gentleman has probably gone quite unraveled through all of this. Watson tries to counter with some dark humor of his own. "One way to look at it, is that you didn't lose your mind and go out and kill yourself, or do anything socially unacceptable ... did you sir?" He lets the smile loose.

Sean's grins and replies, "There was a close call or two, but on a teacher's salary I couldn't afford a long range missile that will reach Tallahassee." Immediately he is sorry he said that, but Watson seems to appreciate the outrageous answer.

"Ha! Ha! Ha! Ha! Yes, that's right. Of course, you're a professor at CSC. Oh believe me, I have been reading about all of the cost cutting changes your new board of trustees is trying to make. It's happening to education all over the state, and it's a darn shame in a lot of ways."

"Shameful indeed," McDuff agrees, still grinning.

"You know, Doctor McDuff, a few of our nurses earned their degrees over there. It's a very good little school I hear, probably the best kept secret in south Florida."

"Thank you, Doctor Watson." Sean is visibly restless now, and trying to control a rising elation. I need to go home, he tells himself. "Not to be rude or short, Doctor, and I thank you for your candidness and understanding, but is there anything else I should know right now?"

Watson slaps his thighs and stands up, reaches out for another handshake, and McDuff stands up and complies. "No sir. You are good to go. Please call me if you have any questions, afterthoughts, whatever."

"Thank you Doctor, I will." Sean is out the office door hurriedly, down the corridor, out the main door of the facility, into the parking lot, into his non-exploding vehicle, and within minutes is pushing the speed limit eastbound on Alligator Alley.

———————

One of the things about rebirth, about stumbling back from the brink of the canyon of death, about a new lease on life, about the bad call being reviewed and reversed, about those doors to love and excitement being slammed shut on your face but then reopened, about good news in general, is that it makes you thirsty. Fortunately for those reborn in McDuff's niche of south Florida, only a mile up county road 86 toward the college, Sean's home, and those reputedly haunted niches of the swamp, is the Muskogee Beverage Center. Sean pulls in, walks quickly to the beer aisles, grabs a six-pack of Irish stout to accompany dinner, and some cherry wheat brew for dessert. One place over from his check-out he sees a tall woman, long raven hair, and he thinks of Jane Green.

The short Seminole man at the check out hands the woman a plastic bag and says, "Have a nice day, Kowechobe."

"You too, Sam." It IS her.

"Hey, Jane," Sean says loudly. She turns to see him and her face lights up in smile and surprise.

"Doctor McDuff!" Jane glances through the store's front windows to the parking lot, then back to Sean. "I'll wait outside for you, OK? I have some news."

"Yes. Great."

After paying for his beers, he quickly goes through the automatic doors and walks over to Jane, standing by her, yes, green vehicle.

"Hi there," he gushes.

"Hi yourself," she replies with enthusiasm.

McDuff goes quizzical for an instant and says, "Jane, before I forget, what did that clerk call you? Kowe ... something?"

"Kowechobe," she smiles. "That's my old legal last name. It's Seminole for *panther.*"

He squints and grins. "That's a great word, name. Why did you change it? When?"

"Oh I did it before signing up for the military. I couldn't stand even the thought of them messing it up on my name tags and things, and on my papers, let alone the mispronunciations that were bound to happen."

"Really? Good thinking. Ha. Ha. But what did your family think?"

"Well, I didn't tell my sisters. And when I told mother she was disappointed at first. But I explained to her that I didn't want to see the family name disrespected and all that, by a bunch of stupid soldiers. She's OK with it now. As for dad, nothing much registered with him back then. I think mom persuaded herself that the name change was like getting married, married to the white man's war machine or something."

McDuff nods and grins and says, "That's a great little story. It really is," still nodding. "Jane Panther, is it? You get more impressive every week."

"Oh boy," she rolls her eyes and laughs. "And you, professor, get easier to impress every week."

Touché, Sean says to himself, then to Jane, "So tell me, what's the news?"

"Oh, I got a letter from Gulf Coast today and I'm a scholarship finalist, which I hope means that I've been accepted at least."

He beams, starts preliminary arm raising for a hug, but with a six-pack in each hand he has to abandon the move, drops the hands to his side again. Jane seems to notice his bungling, and embarrassment, and giggles. Sean recovers with, "Consider yourself hugged, Miss Green. That is good news, and I'm very very happy for you." Goddamnit, he tells himself. This must be one of those signs that I should quit drinking.

"Oh I hope so," she finally says, leaning back against her vehicle now. "So, are you enjoying the break?"

"Uh ... well, yes ... more than I had anticipated, that's for sure."
My god, he thinks. How do I even begin to get into that, assuming
she ... Oh, what the hell. "Let me give you the short version for now. I
can see you are on a mission."

"Oh, this." She holds up the bag containing a bottle. "This is
mother's quarterly ration of cherry brandy. She's home now, and feeling much better, although not back to running the souvenir shop yet.
But my cousin can handle it."

"Ah Jane, that's something I'm glad to hear too, that your mother has recovered," and he nods. They make eye contact, relaxed now,
and pleasantly curious.

"So, yes, my break. I've just come from the clinic with a clean
bill of health."

Jane frowns slightly, nods, grins again and says, "And so?" She
senses there is more to it.

"Well, last summer I was diagnosed with a terminal condition,
and given about a year to live, and I find out today that they were,
pardon the word play, dead wrong ... I mean, they really got it wrong.
I'm fine and dandy, but of course a tad stressed."

A look of horror and awe comes over Jane Green's face, and she
nearly drops her bagged bottle of brandy. "Oh my god," she finally lets
out, turning quickly to open her car door, then putting the bag on the
driver's seat. She closes the door, turns to Sean, takes two quick steps
and hugs him. "I'm so sorry for what you must have been through.
You know," she says as she pulls back now, "Oh my god, you never
seemed to let on. How did you get through this, by yourself? Did any
other faculty know? What about your friends, family?"

McDuff takes a deep breath and laughs softly. "So much of it is
already like a bad dream, mostly. I ... I still don't know."

Jane's demeanor becomes even more serious and concerned, "If
you want to talk more ... I mean, I wasn't planning on going straight
to mother's place."

"No. No. It's OK, Jane. I think I'm coming around pretty well
all ready." He's not so sure now that he should have unloaded something so terrifyingly personal (or that unfolds so) on his student, albeit a former student, and one set to graduate. It's not her problem,

he tells himself. Maybe when I can sort it all out more clearly, and somehow get rid of that car without killing anyone. Jesus, if she knew it all ... hell, I couldn't blame her for calling the police, the FBI. But I can't just slam a door on her that I have opened wide.

"Are you sure," Jane asks. "You know sir, I was in and out of combat zones for a couple of years, and saw a lot of pressure and emotions I'll never forget. And if nothing else, well, I have pretty sturdy shoulders." She gives him an assuring smile, one that only a lifelong friend might be able to muster.

Sean feels a surge of relief, of something especially warm and healing, something he needs in order to get better ... and he returns her smile. "Thanks very much, Jane. Yes, I would like to tell you the whole insane saga some day. But I'll need to hash over some things in my mind and get it right. I don't want to scare you away, or make you sorry you ever asked." He begins to fear that a premature information ball may be in motion, and Jane picks up on this. She hugs him again, this time a longer, stronger embrace, then backs up and leans on her vehicle again.

"Is it OK if I stop by your office some afternoon, in a week or so?"

"Yes. Absolutely," he replies quickly. "I'd like to talk more, when my mind has settled, digested it all, and maybe repented for my crazy turns of thought."

Now she gives him a playful grin, turns and opens her car door and gets in. "Deal," she declares. "I'll be in touch. I promise."

As she pulls away, McDuff's eyes begin to water a little. Then a sudden sober thought in the key of caution: This young woman is a student nevertheless. I'm old enough to be her father, if I'd had a kid at twenty or so.

12

Happy Hour Redux

During the week following spring break Sean and Barry try the happy hour at Fungoola Fred's and catch up, but not completely. McDuff is still not ready to tell his colleagues, even the best one, about the false positive that nearly brought about a very big and ugly negative. The largest of the negatives can never be revealed. But Barry is quick to see that Sean's demeanor, his attitude, is more up-tempo than it has been in months. He attributes it to the defeat of the migraines, and is glad to have his informal mentor back. And there's something McDuff wants to know.

"How did the Key West junket with Miss Rollins go, Barry? Any dirt I should not know about?"

Hope throbs with laughter and replies, "Oh, good doctor, we had a ball! No. Wait a minute. I should clarify that before visions of colleague coitus dance in your head. We drank and laughed a lot, slept in separate beds, but the weekend was not devoid of close calls."

"Well, you are an honorable and boring couple who should be around here a long time, if the gators don't get you."

"Or the pythons," Barry adds. "My neighbor cornered a twelve-footer in his backyard last week, probably sniffing around for his Yorkie."

"Wow. A constrictor that big could kill a full grown man. What did he do about it?"

"He called animal control, and they called the county game warden, and he called in the park rangers. They told some guys who are commissioned by the state to trap and kill the things. That's the report I got."

"Hmm. That explains what I saw on the news last night."

"What's that?" Hope can feel one of McDuff's politically incorrect lies coming.

"The governor was filmed dedicating that multimillion dollar business complex building near Orlando, and he was clearly wearing new snakeskin boots."

"Aah," Barry responds, raising his mug of draft as if to toast. "The man's a real hero who really knows how to make a statement."

Inevitably though, discussion sinks to a rehash and comparing notes on the recent board of trustees meeting. Sure enough, the VP/ EP objects to certain individuals who have cut the college mustard and are moving up the ladder, as Barry is. M.C. Bodey, in all of his trumpish arrogance, signature navy blue sport coat and shiny white pants, loudly agrees, on the grounds that a good business needs to scrutinize more carefully all of its decisions that involve spending more money. In fact, Bodey adds, the entire promotion and tenure concept, and whether the weak work loads and vague performance standards for teachers justify such pay increases, will be coming under the microscope at the next board meeting. He concludes by praising the VP/EP for his courage and insight into such a crucial matter, adding that CSC needs more business sense administrators like him.

But as McDuff predicted, Clarise Robbins, the only veteran board member left over from the good old days, calmly brings to the attention of the meeting that they do not have authority to reject in this case the decision of the college to promote, or award tenure. They are required by law to simply sign off on it, in accordance with state regulations. She even reads the law to them from a thick folder of statutes and such, adding that if they do not approve the paperwork, they leave themselves wide open for a lawsuit by the affected faculty members. Attorney Robbins concludes by suggesting that, "What CSC needs are a few more administrators that can read and respect the law." It's a quote that, during following weeks, mysteriously appears scrawled on numerous note cards tacked to hall bulletin boards in the faculty office building.

"Dean Wiggins stopped me yesterday and congratulated me on my promotion," Barry tells Sean. "He said it will all be reflected in my new contract, probably in June."

"Cheers," grins the doctor. They toast.

On the first Monday in April, a day after Fool's Day, Sean sits behind his office desk and fills his briefcase with student essays submitted that morning by his freshman writing class. It's a much smaller class than usual, just over a dozen students, and a good class for a change. At least half of them are within striking distance of earning As, and baring a burnout or a plagiarist no one should do worse than a C minus. Thus he will go home now at mid afternoon not dreading an evening of papers perusal.

But nested in his garage still is Polly Apocalypse, in all of her dreadful potential.

He closes the briefcase, glances up at the office door, and there is Jane Green, smiling and about to knock. Sean breaks into a wide smile, stands, and motions her to enter and shut the door. She does so softly, turns and goes to the chair by the window and sits. McDuff walks around to the front of the desk and leans back on it.

"So glad to see you Miss Green," he says. "What's new, and how's your mother?"

She looks him over with a wide but careful grin, as if checking for bugs on a plant she's thinking of buying. Satisfied that he's a safe bet, she laughs and replies. "I am very well, thank you. And so is mom. And," she squints, "just as important, how are you doing? I get the feeling you are in better spirits than the last time we talked, even though you don't have two bags of beer in your arms."

"Ha, ha, ha!" God that's funny, he tells himself. "Yes, Jane. I'm coming around, after my seven-month tango with the grim reaper; and he's a lousy dance partner I might add." Golly, that's a quick, witty reply. I am coming around.

"I am so glad to see that," Jane chuckles. "Sorry I couldn't check in earlier. The classes and family stuff have kept me busy." She looks down for a second at her jeans, then smiles up at Sean. There's a little hesitation in her voice as she says, " I wanted to call you, but I wasn't sure if I should tie up your office phone and ...."

McDuff reaches to his right and snags a business card off of the top of the desk, picks up a pen and writes his home and cell numbers on the back of it. "Here," as he hands it to her. She takes it from his hand as if plucking a petal from a flower, turns it over and grins widely while reading the information. She seems a little embarrassed now.

Sean barks, "No excuses now, lady! Call whenever and wherever the spirit moves you. I am your ally in future educational endeavors. Got it? And available for counsel twenty-four seven. In addition," he hesitates now, as to whether it's appropriate, as to whether she might take it poorly, whether he is about to reverse inertia. "In addition, Miss Green," a dash of understated humor may help, "I kinda like you."

She looks down again, chest throbbing in a light laughter of relief it seems; then looks at McDuff with a smile. Her green eyes arrest him for an instant with their joyful glow, and Sean feels as if he has just spoken his truest words in a couple of years. But how much more truth he can get into right now, he is not so sure.

"Yes sir," she finally answers with a sharp nod. She digs in her purse and removes a card, then finds a pen and writes on the back of it. "Here's my cell number Doctor McDuff. Just in case ...."

He cuts her off and says, "You know, Jane. Since you are so close to graduating, and no longer in my class, you can call me Sean, if you're OK with that."

"Well, OK. That probably makes sense. I mean ...."

McDuff senses more uneasiness in her now, and quips, "Or ... I've always liked 'Your Majesty' too, but I'm fine with Sean, if it's fine by you." He notices the inadvertent, awful rhyme and hopes Jane does not. Decent poetry just ain't in you, he tells himself. Now try to dignify the direction of this.

Jane nods again, and smiling says, "So, what do you have to say for yourself? I mean, how's your recovery from the, 'insane saga' I think you called it. How's it working out? I imagine you're still having some aftershocks, and you mentioned how it seemed like a bad dream, that day in the parking lot."

"Jane," Sean has to put the icebreaking wit away, "those are some good questions. Almost sounds like you have some therapy experience, and I really appreciate your genuine concern." He takes a deep breath and looks past her and out the window briefly, then into her eyes once more. "I'm still feeling a little beat up, emotionally."

"Well hell yes. You should." She seems much engaged and curious.

"And I have a very big problem at my home that ... well, Jane, honestly I don't think I should unload that on you here. By that I mean, a college office, or rather." He has to think.

A frown of concern comes to her face now. "That's OK, Sean." A pensive look comes next, then she suggests, "Hey, I owe you a beer, so if it's not inappropriate, you know, out of line with any rules of the college ... well." She is still a bit uneasy. McDuff sees, but she is determined to get it out. "I can meet you somewhere, say, a week from Friday if that's not too long, or I mean inconvenient. You know."

McDuff breathes relief, "That's perfect, Jane. Really, that's a great idea. We can do lunch, or dinner if that's more convenient."

A comfortable and happy air takes over the room, and they smile at each other. Some playfulness returns to her voice as she asks, "You don't have to answer this now, but what sort of bad thing did you do when you thought you had nothing to lose? You didn't steal a fighter jet or something from Homestead, did you?"

Sean suddenly feels some uneasiness sneaking up, and counters with the elusive wisecrack, "Aah, Jane. You didn't tell me you were a clairvoyant. But let's just say I'm glad you have Air Force experience. That can help."

"Actually, I'm not a real pilot. I worked with drones, and a few lecherous officers. I was lucky to escape with my limbs, my life, and my female honor. But we won't go there today." She rolls her eyes and shakes her head, as if it's a here-we-go-again chapter she'd like to avoid.

"Aren't drones mainly reconnaissance aircraft?"

She shoots him a playful frown and answers, "Hold it there, friend Sean. I want to hear about your nightmares first. That's the deal."

He laughs and looks down at the floor for an instant, then back at Jane. She is indeed something to behold, he tells himself, a lifeguard in the great whirlpool of life ... something poetic like that.

"Deal. I shall await your call, as to final details of the rendez-vous."

"And I shall await yours in return, if I only reach your voice-mail."

They stand up and hug quickly, briefly. Then Sean moves to the door, opens it, and Jane passes through. Her long black hair, not po-nytailed today, and her tan arms and shoulders, neck, face, gleam like precious metal.

At the doorway of the outer office Jane stops and looks back at McDuff, notices that the administrative assistant is not at the desk, and says, "Bye Sean. 'Talk to you soon."

"Yes, Jane. I look forward to it."

13
Puppies

He turns left out of the shells and sand access road to his home, and heads south on county road 86, a fifteen-minute drive to the college. It might be faster by boat, Sean often thinks, because the road from CSC winds west, southwest, then east back toward the river and Sean's property, then north into sparse wetland and spooky grounds sparsely populated.

Just off the highway, about fifty yards ahead of him, two men in jeans, wearing dark ball caps and white t-shirts, scurry out of the dry drainage ditch and into a brown pick-up truck. The truck fishtails out of the uncut grass, then speeds off down the road.

What the hell are they up to, Sean wonders.

McDuff slows his old Camry as he approaches the departure point of the truck, and glances over to the ditch. He sees something small and squirming, pulls the car over, stops and gets out. Walks closer to what looks like black and yellow wads of fur, then breaks into a trot and exclaims, "Oh come on! Jesus Christ, what sort of low-life cracker-ass stunt is this?"

Two puppies, maybe two weeks old, eyes barely open, roll and whine in the grass. He picks one up in each hand, holds them up to eye level and asks, "Goddamn you two, you two little cuties, what'd you do to deserve this?" The black one screeches, followed by a squeaky howl from its little yellowish comrade. Sean holds them against his chest, turns and walks back to his car. He opens the passenger front door and gently sits them on the floor mat. They whine and squirm more as he shuts the door. He gets back in and starts his engine, checks for traffic (clear), then slowly inches back on to the highway.

Now what, he asks himself. Think Mac. I can't take them to the office. And I have a class in thirty minutes. There's that veterinary clinic and pet boarding place a few miles down the road from the college. Yes. That's the best option.

He pulls the iPhone from his jacket pocket and dials the L & L secretary.

"Language and Literature. How may I direct your call?"

"Carla. Sean."

"Oh good morning Doctor McDuff. How are you feeling today?"

"I'm fine, thank you Carla. But something has come up on my drive to school, and I need a small favor."

"Oh. Have you had an accident?"

"No, no, nothing like that. It's sort of a humanitarian issue I guess."

"What?"

"Aah, I just found a couple of very young puppies in a ditch near my house, dumped there by some scumbags. So I'm going to take them to the vet's office down the road from the college and see if they can do something with them, check them out, find them a home or something."

" Ooh, Doctor McDuff, you are such a good man. Oh, is there anything I can do to help?"

"Yes, yes there is, Carla. There's no way I will make it to campus by eleven, so could you, or one of the student assistants, meet my eleven o'clock class over in room 365 and just tell them that class is cancelled, and to check the course web site tonight for further instructions ... and that I apologize, because I know there are several commuters in the class who drive a ways to get there."

"Oh certainly, Doctor." He can actually hear Carla scribbling down the room number, he assumes, and his further instructions. "Oh, Doctor McDuff, that is such a caring thing you are doing. Is there anything else?"

"No. Thanks very much, Carla. And if anyone needs to see me, just tell them I will be in in about an hour, although maybe sooner, but an hour is a safe guess."

"Of course, sir. And good luck with your, uh, humanitarian issue?"

In fifteen minutes Sean walks in to the waiting room of Anderson Animal Clinic and up to the chest high counter, a puppy cradled in each arm. A middle-aged and chunky brunette, in whites, smiles and stands up to greet him, noticing his small cargo. There are no waiting customers in the room.

"Oh good morning, sir. Aah, let me guess. You found these little guys recently, right?

"Just a few minutes ago, in a ditch a few miles up the road. I saw a truck pulling away when I got on the highway from my house, and stopped to investigate."

She reaches for the yellow one and McDuff hands him (maybe her) over gently. She strokes the puppy on its head and says, "They look to be part lab, and fairly healthy, thankfully. What would you like to do, sir? Would you like the doctor to examine them? Do you want to take them home if they're all right?"

"Honestly, ma'am. I just can't take them in at this time. I'm on my way to work, and a little late now. I was hoping maybe you could call the county shelter, or find a home or an adoption agency. Heck, I don't know. I just couldn't leave them there." He hands her the other puppy and she places the two of them on her sprawling desk, where they seem to relax and whimper a little.

"That's OK. I understand. But we don't want to send them to the county. They wouldn't last long there, if you know what I mean?"

He truly doesn't know what she means, but nods in understanding anyway.

"Here's what we'll do. Doctor Anderson will give the puppies a thorough going over, to make sure they don't have anything contagious or dangerous. You know. Then if they are healthy and adoptable, we'll take care of them, even bottle feed them if necessary, and when they're too cute for comfort we'll bring a nice shiny kennel out here in the reception area to keep them in, and display them up for adoption."

Sean is relieved, and impressed. He smiles widely at the woman and says, "Oh, you've just made my day. Thank you. That's great."

"Just don't tell a lot of people that we do this on a regular basis. It could get out of control, if you get my drift."

Her drift eludes Sean as well, but he nods in agreement to her request.

"Sir, what I do need to ask you for though is your name and contact information, in case there's an issue with the animals involving ownership or anything, I mean possible previous ownership. Don't worry, it's extremely unlikely that we will need to call you about anything. It's never happened before. But Doctor Anderson likes to cover all the bases just in case. There is little or no chance that the people who abandoned these animals are going to come through that door at a later date looking for their dogs. And if we have proof that they may have originally abandoned them in such a callous way, well, we are not obliged or required to return the puppies."

McDuff removes a business card from his wallet and hands it to the woman.

She reads it and exclaims, "Oh my goodness! You're Doctor McDuff, from the college!" She reaches out for a handshake. "Oh, Doctor McDuff I am so happy to meet you," as she shakes his hand enthusiastically. "I'm Patsy Benson. My son Brad took your writing class his first year at Cypress, and he just loved it."

"Really? Brad Benson. Yes. I remember Brad. That was four or five years ago, wasn't it?

"Five long years. And now he's working over in Miami as an accountant. I should really thank you for, well, really turning Brad on to college. He went there a little reluctantly, and the idea of having to take a doggone writing course just, well, you know."

Goddamn, McDuff admits to himself. That's three things in the last minute that I don't really know.

A short and husky fortyish man in blue scrubs walks into the receptionists' area, then grins at the puppies on Miss Benson's desk.

"Oh, puppies," he observes. "What are we doing here?"

"Oh, Doctor Anderson. Please meet Doctor McDuff, from the college. He found these poor kids in a ditch near his house, and rescued them."

Anderson gives Sean a good visual once-over, as if he's a patient. Then his face lights up and he asks, "Sean M. McDuff? You're the man who wrote that funny book on fishing several years ago, right?" Then the veterinarian offers a handshake.

"Yes, I'm afraid that's me."

"Well I'm pleased to meet you Doctor McDuff. Loved your book. Probably read it three times, in the first couple of years it was out. Laughed my butt off every time. I even bought a copy for my former colleague up in Bradenton, Doctor Suarez. He's a real sportsman, or so he thinks. One of those guys that goes up into Canada a couple of times every summer and fishes for wild trout. He does those trips where they drop you off by plane, then come back for you in a week or so."

"That's some serious angler friend you have there Doctor Anderson. How did he like the book?"

"Ha, ha! Not nearly as much as I did. Sometimes he can't take a joke."

Sean chuckles and replies, "Well, I'm afraid there's still some of that going around."

"Hey. Since you're here, and if you have a minute. Would you mind signing my copy of *The Compleat Masochist*? It's on a shelf in my back office? I'll go get it."

"No problem, Doctor Anderson. Be happy to."

The vet bolts from the reception area and is back in less than a minute. Meanwhile, his assistant is picking up the puppies. She cradles one in each arm and rocks side to side, humming something unfamiliar to McDuff. Doctor Anderson opens the book to the title page and passes it over the counter to Sean.

"Charles. No, make it out to Chuck."

McDuff writes, *for Chuck, an avid angler, and an even better doctor ... may all your fish be big ones ... Best, Sean McDuff ... April 2012.* He hands over the book to its owner, and Anderson opens it again, reads.

A large smile comes, and he says loudly, "Beautiful! That's great. Can't wait to show this to Manuel. Thanks again doctor."

"No. Thank you, doctor, especially for taking the puppies."

"Happy to help."

"Well, I need to get to the college. Thank you both, again."

Doctor Anderson just grins and waves good-bye.

Well, says Sean to himself as he gets into his car, I'm glad I did that. A sign that my soul is on the mend ... that my heart is beating, in tune? Huh? Still though, there's Polly.

———

"Welcome Doctor," says Carla, as Sean enters the outer office area of his department headquarters. "How are the puppies?"

"Doctor Anderson at the animal clinic is going to check them out, then put them up for adoption at his office. I'm relieved. Any messages, Carla?"

"Oh, I'm so happy to hear that. You are a saint, Doctor. And by the way, your students were very cordial and attentive. Not too overly excited that class was cancelled. Oh, and no, no messages."

McDuff nods, smiles and enters his office. "I need to log an office hour, for old time's sake," he mutters. He sits in the chair by the window and turns it to face looking out across campus. The Tower of Babble is still there, and beyond that the hammock that borders the wetlands and river. His thoughts turn to Jane Green, and what to say next.

Guess I'll start with revisiting my prolonged grief, and trust she'll understand and sympathize. Whether my added disgust with the job is enough to justify a mass murder and suicide, damn, that's stretching it. She already knows that I thought I was dying anyway. I'm sure she knows about Sarah. Hell, the whole college knew it the next day. But bombing the school? How do I connect those dots? How do I tell her I almost killed her, albeit unintentionally?

Then an even bigger horror hits him again, her letters of recommendation. What if I had done it, and there she sits with reference letters from a mass murderer? Oh shit.

He rubs his forehead with his right hand.

Maybe I should just forget the whole confessional with her. Just put her off, turn a cold shoulder. She's very bright. She'll get the message quickly. She'll go away sooner or later ... off to grad school ... save the Everglades.

———

When McDuff gets home from campus on Thursday afternoon he notices the blinking green message light on the kitchen phone. Maybe that's Jane finally, he wonders. Sure enough, "Hi Sean. It's Jane. Sorry I took so long to get in touch, but the smoke has finally cleared from a long week of classes and course papers. How about meeting me at Poopdecks, you know, our old hangout, tomorrow about four thirty? I really want to hear about your recent ordeals. So let me know if tomorrow is OK for you. See you soon I hope. Bye."

"... our old hangout," he chuckles to himself.

McDuff presses the return call button. After six rings the great game of phone tag begins: "Hi. It's Jane. Sorry I can't take your call. But please leave a message and I'll get back."

Well crap. "Yes. Hi Jane, it's Sean. Tomorrow, four-thirty, Poop-decks. Confirmed. Looking forward to seeing you again."

Click.

So much for cool rejection, he says to himself. Besides, she deserves better than a cowardly voicemail.

He goes to the refrigerator and takes out some leftovers for his dinner: the remaining half of a baked chicken breast, from last night; mashed potatoes, a puddle of gravy from a jar centered on the fluffy serving; day-old steamed asparagus. He places them (in their plastic storage containers) on the counter next to the microwave, then goes back to the fridge.

"Yum," he smiles, and removes a cold bottle of Guinness. "Think I'll have my vitamins."

14
Poopdecks

The waitress seats Sean and Jane in a corner booth of the rickety restaurant, many stations away from the few other customers. Jane wears white jeans and a black, tight-fitting, sleeveless v-neck top tucked smoothly into her jeans; McDuff khakis and yellow, short sleeves sport shirt, untucked. They look appropriately casual for the place, and also happy to be there.

For starters they order a couple of beers, Dogfish Head, and cups of clam chowder.

Jane begins the serious part with, "You know, Sean. And this is going to sound awfully strange, and if it's not something you want to talk about just say so ... but I'll bet that if I'd known your wife I would have liked her a lot."

McDuff is surprised by this. He just looks down at the table for a moment, nodding. Then he smiles. If any other woman he knows only casually would say such a thing, his response would be something to the tone of, oh really, and what in the hell gives you that idea?

"Yes," he replies. "I do think you two could have become friends. You have very similar senses of humor, wit. Both really darn smart, inquisitive, even sensitive."

Yes, she's right, he admits. So Sean begins to lightly reminisce through some of the highlights of his marriage, but not sadly so. Perhaps that sappy proverb of his mother has finally sunk in: Don't cry because it's over; smile because it happened. Best part, Jane clearly enjoys the anecdotes and domestic yarns too, all through their meal and into dessert.

They order two more beers. Then Jane risks it: "I can only imagine, and probably not so accurately, how much her death brought you down. I know when my grandmother, well, went away, well, we were very close. There were times, off and on for a few years really, I felt like ending it all, even when I was only about ten."

"You probably do have a pretty good feel for that level of grief, Jane. How did you hold up at the funeral?" Oh man, why in the world did I ask her that?

She grins. "That's the strange part," she says. "There wasn't a traditional funeral, because there was no body."

"Huh?" McDuff envisions fatal gore at the hands of a giant alligator, a huge black bear, panthers.

"She just disappeared into the wetlands, by her own design, and was never seen again. No remains. I remember her telling me a month or so beforehand that she was bound for The Mother, whatever she meant by that I'm still not completely sure. Search parties turned up nothing."

Sean transitions back into the suicide side bar, and tells Jane he was in fact on the verge of doing himself in, and a bunch more, then something happened.

She gives him an understanding frown, then asks, "When was that?"

He hesitates, turns away for a short moment, then faces her. "About a month ago."

He is relieved that she doesn't look shocked. She just takes a deep breath, then says, "I think you are over it now, the suicidal thoughts I mean. And I'm glad."

"Indeed I am. I really am. When I, well, came to my senses I guess, I was scared shitless of myself for a while. I even cried a little." Oh man, how much farther can I take this?

"I'll bet, but why were you going to kill others too," she inquires, sincere curiosity in her eyes now. "Who?"

"That's the part that bothers me the most, not because they weren't deserving of something terrible, but ... but, hell, because it was suddenly mortifying to realize how low they had helped to render me with their underhanded idiocy. I ... I was embarrassed beyond ... hell, I still can't even put it into the right words, Jane." Yes, it's a bit of a dodge, but also true he tells himself.

She shakes her head and smiles, and with the fingers of her right hand covers her lips for an instant, glances down at her mug of brew, then over to McDuff, who is now taking a drink of his beer.

"Well well," Jane sighs, "do you mind telling me who those terrible people were, and how you were planning to rub them out, hit man?"

Her word choices, and almost whimsical tone, clue Sean that maybe she doesn't really expect an honest answer, at least not yet. And for that he is grateful. He's dumped enough on her for one evening, and opened enough of his own wounds for now. Time to lighten the load and finish on a high note.

"Aah no, my trusty maiden. For answers to those questions and more, you will need to lure me into another rendezvous, at a future date, er, I mean time. Do not ever call it a *date*, lest we find ourselves in the campus stocks come Monday morning, for violations of student/teacher etiquette."

"Oh curses, my lord," as Jane feigns heartbreak and disappointment, "then you should consider killing those judgmental pricks too!"

Instead of quipping that he almost did McDuff breaks into hysterical laughter, and Jane follows. Light chat ensues, for a few more minutes, then Sean pays the tab. Jane leaves the tip, as she insists. They stroll hand in hand (mutually initiated) out into the parking lot, over to Jane's car.

They embrace, as Sean kisses her lightly on the cheek, then pulls back to look her in the eyes, their green glow remarkable in the half-light of the south Florida night.

"Thank you so much Jane, for a much-needed, very nice evening."

"Mutual thanks to you too," she replies. "And here's an idea. How about we try this again a week from Sunday, Earth Day? I'll be on campus ten to noon working one of the Student Green Team tables, selling stuff to raise money for various Everglades conservation causes. I'll call you when I'm done."

"You won't need to call. I'm planning to be there, never miss it."

"Great. Then, we'll just figure something out then, for the afternoon? It's my turn to treat."

"OK. Sounds like a solid plan," he replies, hands on her waist, face beaming.

She hugs him, and kisses his cheek.

The hugs cease and they part.

When she gets to the main road leading to Alligator Alley, Jane Green stops her happy humming of snips of favorite tunes and says to the little ceramic turtle seated on her dashboard, "Yep. He's definitely on the short list, very short endangered species list, for serious new best friend. And he's awfully darn cute too."

———

"Earth Day, Yay," Sean spouts loudly as he pulls his Camry into the nearly empty faculty parking lot. He notices the meager early turnout, and writes it off as just another case of bad timing, what with finals and graduation only a week or so away. On the other hand, he notes, it's eleven thirty. He starts walking.

He rounds the faculty office building and heads toward the quadrangle. The gathering is just fifty yards away now, and there looks to be maybe a hundred people variously scattered among a half dozen tables and tents. At a table on the far end of the festivities he sees Jane Green and picks up his pace. When he is within fifty feet of the group there, Jane sees him, waves enthusiastically and shouts, "Doctor McDuff! Welcome to Earth Day!" It brings a broad grin to his face.

"Aah, Miss Green. Nice to see you. How are you doing on this bright spring morning. You are looking chipper." And that's a huge understatement, he remarks to himself. She is wearing white gym shorts cut about two inches below her buttocks, and a bright green silk halter top that gives her flat abs plenty of room to enjoy the sunshine, plus some breathing room for her smooth cleavage. Her hair is pulled back in a clean, long ponytail, and she's wearing gold hoops earrings.

She motions him closer, then places the back of her right hand by the left side of her mouth in the classic secret-telling posture. He instinctively leans in to her.

"This is my rarely worn arch sleaze attire," she whispers. "It's supposed to bring in more guys, in hopes that they'll buy more of our modest wares. The other girls talked me into it. Please bear with me, no pun intended, for about another half hour. I brought a decent change of clothes that I can't wait to get into before we sneak out of here."

McDuff begins to throb with laughter. "Yes ma'am. I respect your clever capitalist tactics, informed by Doctor Freud no doubt." He backs away a few steps, still laughing. Then he sees Barry Hope over by the veggie burger stand, waving at him. "I'll be back promptly at quitting time. Noon, right?"

Jane smiles widely and says, "Noon," and points a finger at him.

He strolls over to Barry, grinning all the way.

"Barry!"

"Doctor!"

They shake hands. Then the young instructor puts a hand on Sean's shoulder and asks, "If I may be so curious, who IS that incomparable goddess you were just speaking with? If she's a student here, how the hell have I missed her?"

"Oh her?" McDuff glances back over to Jane's table. "She's just a former student. Had her in a couple of classes over the years. She's very bright. Nice girl, actually woman. She's an Air Force veteran, graduating this term, then probably headed for grad school in the fall, I think she said."

Barry Hope senses that his colleague is holding back, but has the good taste and sense to leave it at that. Then to the surprise of both, Hope Rollins pops up right in front of them, bouncy and happy to see them it seems.

"Hello there, gentlemen and scholars. Happy Earth Day to you."

Barry responds first, "Hope! I knew you'd make it." They hug.

"Aah, the charming and controversial Miss Rollins," Mac says. "Very nice to see you on an off day."

She curtsies and says, "Why thank you, Fearless Leader. Quite likewise."

Sean laughs heartily and replies, "You have just scored a heap of promotion points madam. Congratulations."

Barry starts looking side to side frantically and asks, "Is there a beer stand here that I've missed?"

They all three are laughing loudly now. These two are first rate outside the classroom too, McDuff observes to himself. More people in this job need at least a dash of their loose wit and candor, and maybe a few blows to the head.

Hope Rollins surveys the activities around them. She pauses to focus on Jane's table, frowns cherubically, then asks, "Where do you suppose the Student Green Team got the money to bring in that supermodel to work their jewelry store?" Sean hadn't even noticed that Jane's table had necklaces and bracelets for sale, donated by her family shop.

Mac and Barry look at each other and laugh again, then Barry quips, "I think the EPA sent her down here to make sure all goes smoothly."

At noon Sean exchanges good-days with Barry and Hope, and strolls back over toward Jane's table. She bends over and pulls a hefty backpack out from under the table as he is walking by, slings it over her shoulder, then catches up with the prof and gives him a soft punch in the arm. They look at each other and smile.

Barry and Hope are watching. Hope punches Barry's arm and says, "OK mister assistant professor, spill the beans, or you're buying me lobster tonight." She grins up at him

"Honest to god, Hopester, I know nothing, nothing! Except that she's his ex-student who's going to grad school in the fall. I don't even know her name. He didn't say."

"Well, good for her," Hope Rollins responds grinning, "and for him."

15

The Other Woman

After Jane ducks into the student union restroom and changes into jeans and a short sleeve tan cotton blouse, they walk to Sean's car in the faculty parking lot. Coincidentally, McDuff is casually decked in Lee's and a khaki Columbia sportsman shirt, one with myriad pockets, and short sleeves. He observes, "We look like we're teamed up for the Bass Masters."

"We'll win too," she jokes.

"Jane, how about the sub shop up the road? Then if you don't mind, and have time, there's something at my place that I really need some professional counsel about, and that you'll need to see." There, he says to himself, I've laid it out as much as I dare right now. I hope she doesn't read it wrong.

She doesn't hesitate, for which Sean breathes relief, and she says, "Great. I'll follow you."

At the little bistro they decide on a to go order, and in ten minutes are back on the road, northbound to McDuff's home.

In another ten minutes they turn into his access road that winds briefly through oaks, cabbage palms, and palmettos, then opens into a largely cleared acre bordering the river, where the sprawling house sits. He pulls into the concrete driveway, but doesn't open the garage door. Jane parks close behind him.

Jane is beaming as she emerges from her SUV and says, "Sean, this is just beautiful. How many teaching jobs are you holding down to keep it up?"

He grins, and lifts the bag of sandwiches and potato salad out of his car. Closes the door. "Thanks. It's my dear departed wife's doing, or rather her very rich grandparents, who left her a lot of money about a decade ago. We built this about seven years back, before Bushdom squelched the development boom that was supposed to occur all around us. I have about ten acres, mostly waterfront. Don't tell any-one." Good to try to ease her into a keep-a-secret mood, he feels.

Sean shows her around the house before they need to break into sandwich. He asks her, "Would you like to eat in the dining room, at the kitchen counter, or in the rec room?"

"Let's do the rec room. I have a feeling that may be where you do your best thinking and communicating."

They go to the rec room, sit at the bar there and unbag their food. Then he gets up and moves to the refrigerator. "How about a beverage," he asks.

"Yes. Yes," she replies. "Water, please."

He removes a couple of bottles of spring water and walks back to his bar stool. He opens them both.

"Thank you, good doctor." She gives him a glowing smile.

While they're eating and chatting he recalls that, at Poopdecks, he forgot to tell her the story about his great puppy rescue. So he does.

She is moved and impressed. He IS a good man, she tells herself. I was right.

Then McDuff's face goes lightly grim, fearful, as reluctance creeps in on him. Jane, meanwhile, is beginning to wonder what sort of "professional counsel" he needs from her. She is about to ask when Sean blurts, "Do you know much about high tech explosives and how to get rid of them safely without hurting anybody?"

She straightens up in the bar stool and leans against its back, frowning slightly, but grinning. A good sign so far, Sean feels.

"Mmm. Go on." Her grin remains.

"Oh Jesus, Jane. There's no smooth transition into this, so here goes."

Her grin is still there, but her eyes tighten and stare at him. McDuff takes a very deep breath.

"Back in February, during the lowest point of my twisted psy-chological depths, I purchased a weapon, illegally you could say, from an old acquaintance from my Army reservist days a long time ago. I was going to blow something up and myself with it. My lingering de-pression over Sarah's death, my own fatal condition, my disgust with the state of my profession ... I was just damn sick of everything, deep down inside. I'm sure no one suspected it though. I suppose I was in the grip of some major dual personality affliction, maybe. Hell if I know, except that when I was alone with my thoughts ... I was just a festering madman bent on destruction, and ending it all." He pauses to rub his eyes.

"OK! OK!" Jane breaks in, holding up a hand as if she's a traffic cop at a busy intersection. He expects her at any second to get up and leave. There is a visible shame and sadness on his face now, and some sternness in hers.

"You don't have to go back there," she reminds him. "Listen. In some different ways, I've been there too ... where you've been ... so I sort of know." She puts her hand down on her thigh. "I'm a friend now. You asked me to help you. Show, don't tell, one of those things you preached in writing class."

McDuff is immediately relieved. He takes another deep breath and stands up. He nods and says, grinning again now, "OK. Follow me. Polly is in the garage."

"Polly?" Jane is puzzled. "You better not have a dead body in there. That would be pushing it, Sean."

Thank god I haven't snuffed her sense of humor, he thinks. This could work out.

They walk through the laundry room and McDuff opens the door to the spacious two point five car garage, as he calls it. They go in as he turns on the overhead lights with the wall switch. Polly Apocalypse sits on the far side behind the John Deere riding mower. She is gleaming red in the sunlight streaming through the sky light vent above her. It's almost holy. They slowly walk over to the vehicle and stand behind it now, about five feet of space between the car's bumper and the main door to the outside, where their respective transportations sit.

Jane breaks the awkward quiet and quips, "Oh Sean. You shouldn't have. You didn't have to get me a new car for graduation."

He laughs softly and thinks, this is going better than antici-pated ... so far. He fishes the keys from his pocket, clicks, and the rear hatch unlocks. He raises it, opens the floor compartment, then removes the false bottom to reveal its top secret stash.

Jane's eyes bulge as she gasps and steps backwards, banging against the garage door. "OH ... MY ... GOD!!" She raises her arms and cups her hands over each temple. "Oh My Fucking God!" She breathes in and out heavily, and looks up at the ceiling, then over to McDuff, confusion, fear, astonishment all over his face now.

She speaks unusually fast, "Sean Sean, I'm so, I'm sorry, I almost never say that word, I mean, Oh Jesus," she backs off the door and does a full pivot, and faces McDuff again. She forces a short laugh, rubs her temples again and goes on, "Oh my god ... Where? No, I don't need to know. I don't want to know. I."

Sean quivers a little, and is unable to respond. My god, he says to himself, my god what the hell have I done here? In a wavering voice he says, "Jane?"

"I'm OK. It's OK," she says, her right hand waving bye-byes to the rear of the Kia, a double gesture. "Close it up, Sean. I get the message. It's all right." She gives him a quick hug. "Let's go back inside. And can I have a drink?"

He closes it up, and they return to the rec room.

Jane sits in the whicker sofa this time. She's regaining her demeanor, her composure, and she says, "I apologize for my outburst. But that's some pretty serious stuff you have there Doctor." Shaking her head she adds, " I haven't seen any of that in a few years, of course, because it's still as far as I know top secret, still in sort of semi-development stages. But that didn't stop the military from trying it out on the enemy in the Middle East, sometimes anyway." She looks away for a second, then smiles up at McDuff, who is standing at the bar filling two rocks glasses with ice and a scarce, eighteen years old Cuban rum, now made in the Dominican Republic, Ron Matusalem. He goes over to Jane, hands her a glass, and sits down on the other end of the sofa. She doesn't ask what it is, immediately takes a long sip.

"Mmm. Thank you," she says. "This is good rum, isn't it?"

He nods and smiles back.

"I had a brief, guilty flashback when I got a faint whiff of the stuff, but nevermind that. It has a faint orangey petroleum smell. Some people can't discern it." Another short sip. "Can you?"

He gives her a quick shake of the head that says **no**. "Jane, I'm sorry, really sorry to drag you over here for this. I had no right to involve you. I really apologize." He looks away at the painting on the opposite wall, a Gauguin reprint of a Tahiti scene. He can't seem to face Jane now.

Jane leans toward him to touch him, but he's out of reach. She sits up straight and replies, "No, I'm sorry I turned into such a drama queen out there. I'm fine now. Let's move on." She sits her drink on the glass center of the wooden coffee table, then says, "You need to get rid of that thing, blow it up as soon as possible, somewhere way off in the swamp." She pauses, then continues, "What sort of detonator do you have? I hope it doesn't have to be triggered in the car."

He faces her now, as some of the regret and uneasiness go away. He tells her that he has a transmitter with about a half-mile range, maybe a little less. She asks to see it, so he goes to a drawer behind the bar and pulls out the device and its battery, brings it back and places them on the table. How in the world does she know all of this, he wonders.

"My sources call it 'the worm,' and it has a safety switch, as does the box under the front seat that is the main detonator I guess."

She just leans over and scrutinizes them, a tiny inquisitive grin on her face now.

"Hmm, yes," she finally replies. "I've heard of these. I really hope your sources are right about the range."

"I guess I'll find out sooner or later. The sooner the better, right?"

"Absolutely," she replies. "Do you have any idea what that substance is? What did your sources tell you? I mean, that explosive, if it's what I think it is, and I really believe it is, it's a closely guarded military secret. If you get caught with it, I'm sure the Pentagon and all of their support groups—CIA, FBI, maybe even the President—would pull every string out there to lock you up for the rest of your life, if they couldn't get away with just killing you instead."

Sean feels panic slinking in now, and his sense of humor going farther south than he can chart. Jane seems a little frantic again. How the hell does she know all of this, he wonders again.

"The lieutenant called it A40."

Jane is quick to reply. "The lieutenant is right. Do you happen to know how he ... no, no ... it doesn't matter. Who in the world is this lieutenant?" She rubs the base of her palm on her forehead, smiles and looks at Sean. "Oh shit, Sean. Nevermind. That's no matter either." She stands up, shaking her head from side to side, a small smile comes to her face and she plops down on the sofa again, staring straight ahead.

To say I've let the cat out of the bag, McDuff tells himself, is the mother of all understatements. Christ, the T-Rex is out of the park.

After nearly a minute of silence, punctuated by heavy, regular breathing, Jane turns to Sean and says, "I'll help you. We can do this. I want to help you with this. We'll do it right ... it might be very interesting." A confident smile comes to her face and her eyes meet his. He sighs and smiles back. Jane goes on, and her tone becomes more leveled and determined.

"Just hang with me for a couple more weeks, OK? Leave Polly where she is, and keep your damn hands off of the worm." She is thinking, planning, focusing. Then she declares, "I AM going to graduate from college first." She slides across the sofa and next to McDuff, hugs him with her left arm, puts her cheek against his chest for a few seconds, then stands up. "And you are required to be there, mister."

Relief flows over Sean, as if he just dropped into a warm bath. He gets up too. "How about another drink," he asks.

"A short one," she replies. "I have to go check up on mother this evening."

They relocate to the bar, and he refreshes their rums.

"There's only one thing you need to be cautious of," she says.

"What's that?"

"If there are thunderstorms in the area, with lots of lightning, get the heck out of here, as far as you can, and keep your fingers crossed. I know there's not much chance your garage would get struck. But ... well, I'll bet you're aware of the consequences."

He smiles and raises his glass to her for a toast. She follows up, and McDuff adds, "Yes, my sources advised me of that as well."

Jane sips, then grins and puts her drink back on the bar. "You know Sean, there's enough there to bring down almost any building in Florida."

He just shakes his head yes, then sideways, as if to reiterate a 'What the hell was I thinking?'

"One more thing," Jane says. "Do you think anyone has any idea that you have this, besides your sources?" giving "sources" the air quotes.

He is quick to say no, and adds, "And believe it or not I feel my supplier, is a hundred percent trustworthy. We are the only others who are aware."

"OK. I think you're right. But I have to say, Sean, ... that's a really nice little van. It's brand new, isn't it? Not the sort of shit your average radical terrorist drives around to blow up embassies, and night clubs."

McDuff laughs and says, "Well, yes. That's the idea I guess. To be less conspicuous. And I could use a new car. But Polly Apocalypse, as her makers named her, is of illegitimate origins. So even without the nasty cargo she could eventually land me in jail, at least."

"Well," Jane says. She sips the last of her rum and claps her hands. "Let's stop speaking of your girlfriend in the garage for now. I'll think of a way, and a place, where we can commit her to the deep swamp with a minimum amount of fuss and attention. And don't worry, Sean. I'm not going to the cops when I leave here, or the feds, or even the old tribal holy men."

She stands, takes a step toward him, and leans over and hugs him while he's still sitting. He puts his arms around her waist and says, "Jane ... I'm not sure how to thank you properly, enough ... I'm not sure I deserve your ...."

The hug breaks up. Both are grinning now.

"Oh heck, I'm not totally sure you do either. But I'm determined to risk it for another few weeks at least. We'll find out."

16
Graduation Day

The days leading up to commencement are easy ones for Sean McDuff, with only a few office hours, mostly devoted to grading two small stacks of take-home finals turned in Monday. On Wednesday he has lunch at the student union snack bar, known affectionately and unofficially as Hell's Kitchen, with Barry and Hope. They tell him of their similar summer plans: teaching an eight-weeks class immediately following the waning spring semester (contrary to the ignorant myth that teachers take all summer off), then visiting their respective families up north, then hooking up for a long weekend at some site on the lower Atlantic coast, yet to be designated.

"Then it's back here for the fall shift at the brain factory," Hope Rollins laughs.

Come Thursday McDuff takes the afternoon off to drive over to Naples. He wants to buy a nice graduation gift for Jane. In addition, a trek into the depths of the wealthy intracoastal neighborhoods reinforces his few-regrets and strong belief in his chosen livelihood. There are homes there with ten thousand dollar front doors, and tied up in their back canals are yachts bigger than Sean's house. Polly could have a feast.

When he returns home from his road trip he sees the blinking green message light on the phone.

"Hi Sean it's Jane, and I just want to remind you that you are required to attend my graduation this evening, and please make some time available afterwards because I have a possible mission for Polly that we should discuss. OK? Oh, but you don't need to bring Polly tonight, OK? Also, feel free to buy me a drink somewhere later if you still like me. Bye Bye. See you soon. Oh, and we can just meet first at the reception in the gym following the ceremony. OK? Bye sweetie."

Sean chuckles as the message ends. That's great, he tells himself. She sounds cheerful and anxious, and I guess she should be. She's graduating *summa cum laude*, and if she wants to she can walk out of there tonight with a former professor of the year and reformed madman in tow. Whatever.

So, she's been thinking about my Polly problem. She really is quite a woman, quickly becoming something, something of a lucky charm, to say the least. And my goodness, her military experiences ... she must have been involved in some very high tech, top secret stuff. Damn if I'm going to ask though.

———

Following the graduation ceremony, a few hundred various participants–graduates, their families, faculty and staff, even administrators–gather in the nearby campus gym for an informal reception featuring free fruit punch in large glass bowls, canned or bottled soft drinks in tubs of ice water, and a selection of yummy fresh snacks catered by the local T.G.I Friday's. Sean is there for fifteen minutes (cap and gown off and ditched in his nearby office) before Jane strolls in beaming, bouncing, glancing all about for her blooming friend. Since she is six-feet tall (as he is) but still bedecked in cap and gown, it only takes her seconds to spot him over the bustle and joy. They both begin a fast walk, weaving, dodging a human obstacle course of very happy folks, and close the forty feet between them in record time. At the point of their union a very long embrace ensues.

"Oh, I'm so glad you're here," she says, the hug continuing, accented now with some left to right motion, enthusiasm.

"Nothing was going to keep me from your big day. I'm happy for you, very, very happy." It's a borderline tender moment, McDuff feels, and many must be noticing by now. Most probably think I'm her father. I'm old enough.

As the hug breaks Jane begins to wipe little tears of joy from her face.

Sean feels something similar coming on, but quells it with, "Jane, you look so lovely, and deserving, and, well, Congratulations!"

She sniffles and laughs, smiling wide, and replies, "Oh, thank you doct ... Oh Sean! Thank you. As strange as it sounds, I may not have made it without you." She laughs and hugs him again.

"Aah Jane. I think you would have, but I feel very good to be a small part of it. Thank you too." He looks past her for a second, then asks, "Is your mother here, family?"

Jane removes her cap and replies, "Oh heck, mother is real sick again ... came over her suddenly last night ... the breathing problems again."

McDuff feels cold and sad, and says, "Jane, I'm so sorry. Do you need to get back?" He hopes not.

"Oh no. It's OK. One of my sisters is down from Orlando, and she's staying with mom. I'm sure they were planning on coming. I was over to visit them this morning, and they seemed very down about mom's situation. She is too sick to attend. Nel told me not to worry, to enjoy the moment, have a good time with your friends, she said. And she also made a point to say how sorry she was that she couldn't come. The best part is that I really think she was disappointed."

Sean recalls Jane telling him a while back that she and her sisters did not get along. So this could be a breakthrough in family dynamics.

They make their way to the beverage tables, look into the slushy reddish punch bowl, then into each others eyes.

"How about Fungoola Fred's? My treat," the professor suggests. "Meet you there!"

———

By nine o'clock the late Friday dinner crowd at Fred's is thinning. Jane and Sean are finishing their dinners, and a bottle of good champagne. Jane looks down to her right wrist, where she wears the gold bracelet that Sean gave her at the outset of their evening there, her graduation gift. It is about two inches wide with three turtles across its top, a small emerald embedded in each of their shells.

Jane smiles and says, "I just love this, Sean. I guess you noticed my affection for turtles."

"Yes," he grins. "I noticed your necklace, and the little earrings you sometimes wear ... and that little guy on your dashboard."

After the waitress clears their plates Jane says, "OK. Are you ready to hear my Polly plan?" McDuff nods. They both glance around to gauge the distances between them and the nearest other diners. It's safe.

Jane begins, first telling him about some sacred Native American burial grounds about ten miles north of his property and just off of the county road. Until the big flood several years ago, that decimated most of it, scattering old bones for about a mile up and down the riverbank, and an acre or so inland, the grounds were protected from hungry developers by county and state statutes. She thought, she says, that they still are, but apparently some big money and underhanded politics recently reversed that status, behind the backs of a Seminole group lobbying for continued protection, and just last week M.C. Bodey Enterprises quietly moved in a lot of heavy equipment to begin major clearing as early as late next week.

"That goddamn Bodey," Mac says. "I'm not surprised."

"Yes," Jane says. "His company had something to do with influencing the relocation of the reservation community near there a while back, after Hurricane Andrew leveled half of the southern glades from coast to coast. I guess that's been, gosh, almost twenty years? My grandma died about three months prior to it all. It was a very traumatic year for me, and a lot of my people."

She has Sean's unquestioning attention now. She goes on to note that the old reservation site is still vacant and undeveloped because as it turns out there is another sacred ground bordering it, and just to the north of the site where Bodey and his gang moved in recently. That area, she says, is said to be haunted by ancient spirits, and almost no Seminoles dared walk it, except her grandmother, who considered herself something of a priestess.

"Way back then," Jane remembers, "most of the tribe seemed to hold grandma in awe. Either that or they thought she was crazy, and were just afraid of her."

Sean is mesmerized, but wondering what this has to do with decommissioning Polly Apocalypse. His wonder quickly diminishes.

"So, my handsome friend with the dangerous car, what say we drive Polly up that way tomorrow night to meet the bulldozer family there at the construction site headquarters? The place has no security or surveillance yet, no guards or locked fences. That's coming next week. It's still a fairly remote location up in there, and the closest residents are at least five or six miles away over secondary roads. The equipment is less than a half mile in off the highway, and it's very unlikely there will be anyone at all up that way on a Saturday night, especially with a storm front coming in out of the south southeast, which we will need to monitor."

McDuff is smiling now, in agreement it seems, but has to ask, "How in the world do you know all of this Jane? How sure are you about the location's dynamics?"

She grins and confidently continues. "My cousin Sam, who drives heavy equipment part time for Bodey, told me in passing a couple of days ago. He doesn't like it, but he needs the money. He has a family to support. Sam drove the wide load trailer in there that carried the modular headquarters building, some pre-fab mobile home sort of thing. They don't even have electricity there yet. There's probably a million dollars worth of heavy equipment at the site: three giant bulldozers, a couple of large dump trucks, generators, a pick-up full of chainsaws and hand tools, the works."

Sean looks very pleased, almost relieved, and more happy by the second as he walks it through his mind. He stares across the table at Jane, who is aglow in anticipation, satisfaction, her eyes looking in to his and drawing him closer to home.

"Let's do it, Jane," he finally says to her. "I take it you have it all worked out."

Jane wiggles in her chair like a happy kid at her birthday party. "I drove up there yesterday afternoon and went through the motions, no one around even in broad daylight." She takes a sip of bubbly, then adds, "You follow me in Polly up to the old reservation entrance, which is a little over a mile north of the site, and we'll park my car about fifty yards in off the road and leave it there. Then we'll take Polly to meet the bad guys, and pull her in nice and close. We'll walk north, sort of parallel the river for about a quarter of a mile, then duck down behind some big ole cypress trees. You get out the worm, and ....” She begins to laugh softly, then says, “Why in the world do they call it that? I feel like I'm talking dirty.”

Sean joins her soft chuckling with his own and replies, “But darling, I love it when you talk dirty.” Immediately he buries his face in his hands and shakes his head, then looks up and faces her with a more sober look now. “I'm sorry Jane, really. I couldn't resist that dumb cliché.”

They both glance away for a few seconds, then Jane continues. “All right. We blow up the damn things, then sort of hack our way north through the hammocks–by the way, bring that machete I noticed hanging in your garage–we go north for about a mile until we're parallel again with the old reservation entrance, cut through to the road ... there's some old walking paths around there if I recall, still, so the final few hundred yards where we have to go west back to the county road shouldn't be hard.”

Sean is again mesmerized by her thorough, confident manner. She takes a drink of water.

A mischievous grin is on Jane's face now as she says, “OK. When we get to the highway, what do we do?”

McDuff is unable to answer.

“We look both ways, to make sure nothing is coming, then run to my car.”

Sean starts to laugh once more. Jane joins in for a few seconds, then continues.

“I'm sorry,” she tells him. “But you know I'm dead serious, don't you?”

He knows it. It's in his eyes, and she sees it.

“Now,” she goes on. “The finale is simple. We drive the mile or so across the reservation's dirt road leading west to county road sixteen. It's a narrow, but paved, mostly southbound route that curves back into 86 about a mile north of your property. There's only a handful of rickety residences along it, a tomato farm, and a run down citrus grove or two. Then once we get to your house you have to fix me something to drink and snack on. That's an order.”

Sean McDuff smiles at Jane and lightly nods. "I adore you General Green, and I look forward to serving ... with you, on this mission."

"I like your attitude, sergeant doctor McDuff. But let's go home and get a good night's sleep so we can be serious and focused tomorrow. I'll be at your house by late afternoon. I need to spend some time with mother and sister in the morning."

Some fatigue is beginning to show on both of them. He pays up and they walk out to their respective cars, parked next to each other. A long hug ensues, then Sean says, "I congratulate you again, my favorite college graduate of all time." Then he takes a step back and offers a handshake.

Jane laughs and shakes his hand, then turns and unlocks her door and gets in, starts the engine, rolls down her window, smiles and blows him a kiss.

17

Palmetto Man

At nine a.m., when McDuff awakens, and slowly walks out on to his deck with a morning glass of juice, he notices a great horned owl perched in the top of the oak where Victor used to loom. Yikes, here come the signs again, he thinks. The professor reclines in his lounge chair to take in the morning air, and begins again to rehash what Jane told him last night. It's a damn good plan, he says to himself, as long as no one is around to get hurt, or killed. As long as we're not seen. And if Martin is right, there won't be any evidence to connect me, or her. It will all be vaporized in the explosion. In an off the wall way we'll be helping the environment by preventing those greedy ass-holes from plundering more land ... at least temporarily ... and we'll be kicking Bodey in the wallet hard, sending a message that maybe even he can read. Jesus, I just hope no one gets in the way.

At three in the afternoon Jane Green pulls into Sean's drive-way in her green FJ Cruiser, gets out and lifts two shoulder bags (one black, one camouflage) out of the back seats. She's wearing cut-off denims and a white v-neck t-shirt, no make up or jewelry, and her black hair is up in a bun. She is grinning as she walks up to McDuff on the front porch and says, "Hi there, sergeant."

"Hello to you, dahling," he replies.

They walk inside and he shows her to one of the two guest bed-rooms down a hall from the master and tells her, "Here are your bar-racks. You can put your bags in there, and there's an adjoining bath to the right past the big dresser. She says 'thank you' and goes in. He turns and strolls to the kitchen and sits at the small breakfast table that he rarely uses. In a few minutes Jane joins him and sits down.

"Scared?" she asks grinning.

His face is almost blank, but serious. The gravity of the upcom-ing act is pulling him in now, and he feels like the man in Poe's maelstrom ... just rolling with the natural power, the flow, and becoming one with the force's ambivalent nuances. No fear, but connection now with his beautiful friend that he does not want to lose. He reaches across the table and takes her hand.

"I am intent on doing this," he replies, "and happy I have you to help me."

"Trust me," she says, "we will pull it off without a hitch."

No one since Sarah, or even before Sarah, Sean realizes now, gives me this kind of determined energy, this focus to do something strong and dangerous together, and believe in it.

———

At nine o'clock Jane checks the weather radar one more time on her laptop, then tells Sean it's time to move out. She is changed into jeans and a dark, long sleeve shirt, and also carries night vision goggles and binoculars on a strap over her shoulder. McDuff is similarly attired. He dons an army green fishing vest and puts the worm in a deep pocket, and its battery in another, then velcroes them closed. Then he picks up the sheathed machete from the sofa.

When they reach their vehicles in the driveway she remarks, "The storms look to be about an hour away, maybe a little less, but the full moon will probably hang on until they are almost on us." She hugs him and says, "Just follow me."

They turn right and northbound out of McDuff's access road, and within about five minutes the highway is devoid of all light but that from their headlights, and the occasional pale moonlight. After twenty minutes of sub speed-limit travel Jane slows down and makes a left into a narrow dirt path, it seems, and Sean follows in Polly. She goes slowly for about a hundred yards, then stops and shuts off the car at a spot where the road widens, giving McDuff enough room to turn Polly around cleanly for the trip back down the highway to the construction site entrance, their target.

As they turn back on to the asphalt Sean asks, "I didn't notice a right turn-off near here, did you?"

"Oh yes. Don't worry. I know exactly where we're going."

Sure enough about a mile back down the road Jane tells McDuff to slow it down, and she points to some fresh and wide gouges in the grassy berm of the road.

"There. Turn left here."

He eases Polly across the crushed vegetation. Just inside the tree line a clear, wide dirt course with two fresh ruts cuts through the flattened weeds and brush.

"This is it," Jane says. "Just take her slow for a few minutes."

"How did I miss this on the way up," he asks. She just gives him a grin, then focuses on the path ahead.

They reach a half-acre clearing in a few minutes and ground zero springs up in front of them: three shiny yellow bulldozers and two huge dark dump trucks sit in a tight half-circle around a fifty by fifteen trailer sitting on concrete blocks. There are three generators to the left of the pre-fab headquarters trailer, and a white pick-up truck parked to its right with a dark plastic tarp covering the bulging contents in the vehicle's bed. McDuff stops his little van near the truck and Jane suggests that he pull Polly in close between the dozers and the trailer. He agrees, eases her in, and shuts off the engine, turns off the lights. He reaches under his seat and flicks on the receiver. Then they get out.

"Excellent work, dearie," Jane says. " Now let's head that way." She points in a direction ninety degrees to their entrance, where the undergrowth and trees seem to flicker in the erratic moonlight. North, he assumes, while south southeast of them the sky is dark, with occasional lightning and distant thunder. When they get to the edge of the clearing Jane puts on her night vision goggles and surveys the area ahead.

"OK," she says excitedly. "Just follow me and stay close," removing the glasses and letting them dangle from her neck. "We're going to go in about four hundred yards and veer toward the river, then get down behind some thick trees. Then you put the battery in the worm."

"I'm with you love." I called her *love*, he points out to himself. He can make out a small smile on her face as she moves into the palmettos.

Neither speaks as they trod carefully through the thick vegetation and trees, occasionally lit by moonlight. They use the flashlights sparingly.

In what seems about ten minutes they are within a stone's throw of the glimmering river and standing under a thin canopy of cypress trees. Jane kneels down behind the thickest of the root clusters and motions to Sean. The site behind them cannot be seen. You would never know what was back there.

The moon slips out from a cloud bank as darker clouds to the southeast, flickering and rumbling, close the gap on it. The professor and the graduate can see each other's grinning faces now as they lie down on the dry spring ground and face away from the distant machines huddled in the clearing south. Jane nods. Sean fishes the worm from the vest, then the battery, and installs.

"Ready," he whispers.

"Oh wait," she replies, and reaches in her shirt pocket and removes two pair of earplugs. She hands one set to McDuff and tells him to put them in, then puts hers in. He follows her instructions, then nods to her again. She nods back. They are lying on their sides facing each other as Sean pushes the blinking red !!!!!!! an unbelievable ungodly earth-shaking KLAHBOOM rocks and shakes the woods as trees and every standing object around them bend sharply, instantly northbound from the force of the blast and wind that seem the rebirth of Andrew squared. For a split second the forest swamp and its every detail are aglow in high-noon light, like a gigantic camera flash has gone off. Everything shivers, quakes as if about to be torn from the earth. In an instant the shock waves and wind roar back toward the explosion and the trees and undergrowth snap back, and point toward the origin of a great undoing. All around is a crashing and clatter of debris, myriad unknown objects zip and slip through leaves and branches like a meteor shower come to earth. The back and forth and up and down rushes of wind quickly diminish, until only eerie rustles and pattering are heard ... all in a matter of three or four horrendous seconds.

Sean and Jane lay there in a daze, both breathing very heavily now, their bodies feeling as if they had fallen from trees above hard to the ground. Temporary concussion fallout from the incredible explosion. Stunned disbelief grips them.

After a few seconds they raise themselves to their knees, quivering, and they embrace. Mild shock. Their hearts beat hard and fast. They take out the earplugs and Jane shakily puts both pair back in her shirt pocket.

"OK?" he asks.

She breathes in hard, exhales and replies, "OK. Yes."

"Wow," he adds softly.

"For sure."

After a short minute they help each other up, brush off, and Jane says, "Let's move." She looks to the southeast sky and points. "We've got about thirty minutes until we get a free shower. And I'm thirsty for something besides water."

Sean removes the battery from the worm and deposits them in separate pockets again, as Jane starts toward a thicket of bushes, and what looks like, in the closing darkness, cabbage palms. McDuff follows again.

It's a slow but steady ramble through the night jungle and wetlands, although not yet so wet in late spring. A couple of times Jane uses the night vision goggles to get her bearings, then confidently proceeds. She really seems to know where she is, Sean admits. A regular Jane of the jungle. After about ten minutes of steady walking and increased heavy breathing they come to a small clearing. Sean is about to ask 'how much farther' when Jane stops abruptly and gasps.

McDuff collides softly with her as a deep, low "HOOLOOF!" roars from the shadowy tree trunks and bushes only twenty feet in front of them.

Jane just stares, wide-eyed and aghast, Sean likewise, as dark shock and disbelief freezes them in their tracks.

Their path is blocked by a huge, hairy thing rising eight feet tall up out of the thick undergrowth, towering like a church steeple against the night, its broad muscular shoulders moving slowly side to side, thick long arms raised chest high, and hands half open as if awaiting the whistle to begin a wrestling match to the death. It stares at them with large reddish eyes that seem to pulsate in the flickering light of the approaching storm.

McDuff slowly moves in front of Jane and to her left, clutching the machete with his right hand. He draws it out of the sheath. The creature glares and raises its huge open hands a little higher. Sean now holds the long knife in front of him at waist level.

"Sean, Sean," Jane says. "No! Put the machete down. Do it now Sean. Bend down, lay it on the ground, and step back. Now Sean!"

There is stern power in her voice that seems to come from the night earth itself, like some undeniable law that must not be ignored. He stoops down quickly and lays the machete in the thin grass, straightens up and takes a step backward, his and Jane's shoulders touching now.

"Ahessi," she says slowly, calmly to the huge creature. "Ahessi."

"Holy mother of god," Sean whispers. Then he turns quickly to face Jane, puts his arms around her and kisses her passionately. To his surprise the response is mutual, and when they softly part he says, " I don't want to die without ever having kissed you on the lips."

"Me too," she says, near breathless as they turn quickly to face the gigantic figure again.

It lowers its arms slightly, seems to nod, glares at them still with pulverizing red eyes. The moon makes another brief appearance from behind a gathering ceiling of northbound clouds, giving more definition to the beastly giant, reddish hair, long and thick on its body except for the bulging chest and Neanderthal face. It is awesome, paralyzing ... something out of a scf-fi horror film, myth. Grendel.

The great thing wrinkles its nose, as if sampling the air. It takes two deep breaths, then lets out a slow, guttural rumble, more like a word than a growl.

"AAAH-ET-EES!"

Then it reels away from them, takes three long strides, and disappears creepy quietly into the darkness. Except for the first two crackling steps, no more sound from the creature's exit is heard. But it is definitely gone in a dark, unreal horrifying flash.

Sean and Jane look at each other now, as Jane grins and says, "Quick. Pick up your machete and sheath it. There's a path to the highway not too far beyond those trees to the left." Her tone is urgent, yet strangely calm.

He follows her orders, then asks, "Holy shit, Jane. What the hell?" unable to finish thought or question.

"He won't be back," she shouts.

"How in the world do you know that?" But she doesn't answer.

They soon come to a narrow footpath that takes them quickly out to the county road, very dark now as the storm nears. They cross, then run down the reservation road to Jane's vehicle, get in, and she starts the engine and pulls out. It begins to drizzle and she says, "We did it my good friend. We did it, but not without a little unexpected ...." She laughs and looks over to McDuff, then back to the narrow dirt road.

He wonders if she is in shock ... the awesome blast, the ... with the ... what?

"Jane, what the hell was that? You seem not so ... like you refuse to ... or acknowledge or ... Goddamn, love, are you OK?" Oh hell I said it again.

She chuckles, and shakes her head. "That," she yells, "is confirmation, finally, of my grandma's genius! Palmetto Man!" She slows down, then turns left on to a narrow, paved road.

My beautiful young genius has lost her mind, McDuff thinks. Seeing such things, creatures, ghosts, are known to do that to you. And what about my head?

Jane's SUV moves steadily down the rough and smallish road into an increasing rain. Wiper blades clack at high speed. Sean just stares cautiously ahead mulling, mulling, hoping the night has nothing more in store for them in the way of shock and awe. Jane's expression seems to mimic that of her friend in the passenger seat, but with a slight grin again.

In about fifteen strangely speechless minutes they arrive at the intersection with county road 86, Jane goes right, as the rain reaches deluge intensity.

"Wow," McDuff observes once more. "This should take care of any fires the explosion may have started." He pauses, then muses,

"And that skunk ape probably needs a good shower." Forced guffaw follows. He is still rattled, drained, but oddly alert.

Jane is quick to reply. "Not a skunk ape. That's mostly the white man's version." She is smiling, mulling it seems as well, but focused on the very wet road ahead.

White man's version, Sean repeats to himself. What the hell does that mean? Oh, I'll leave it until we get home.

Within a few minutes they ease into the McDuff driveway, open their respective car doors and run to the front porch. They stop there and before Sean can get his keys out to open the front door Jane throws her arms around him and they embrace and begin to breathe more easily.

"We did it! Oh, Sean. We did it."

"YOU did it my dearest. You were the brains and nerve that drove the mission. And I can't thank you enough."

"Maybe, but you can at least try by pouring me something to drink. Inside."

He unlocks the door and they rush in the house and out to the kitchen, where Jane sits down at the table there. Sean continues to his bar in the rec room and comes back in a minute with a tray holding glasses, ice bucket, bottles of water, and a tall bottle of sipping rum from Panama called Zafra. He pours, they toast, and McDuff begins. "Not to downplay our gloriously successful act of espionage, but what in the goddamn world ... aah, hell Jane, you know!"

Jane is grinning again and nodding her head up and down. She seems as if she is just coming out of a meditation, collecting her dreamy data and recollections, and carefully wondering, a circling osprey trying to choose a perch from the water below. She slips the picks out of her hair, then shakes her head as the gleaming black tresses fall out and cascade down her torso, nearly reaching her waist.

Sean asks, "Were you talking to that thing? Did it talk back to you? What in the hell ... and what's your dear deceased grandmother have to do with it?"

She finally looks Sean in the eyes and answers, "Oh god, Sean. I hardly know how to tell it. Where to start."

She's exhausted, he notices. I won't press her.

But she begins.

"That meeting, encounter, after the explosion ... I immediately flashed back to things my grandmother used to tell me, when I was eight, nine, ten even. And that may have saved us." She sips on the rum and goes aah, then continues. "One of the reasons a lot of the people on the reservation thought grandma was a little off her rocker is that she sometimes talked about what she saw and did on her two or three-day wanderings into the wilderness near there, actually very close to where we were tonight. And grandma's favorite tales involved a family of palmetto people she claimed to have befriended, and carried on a relationship with, off and on for ... heck, at least ten years I guess."

"Palmetto people?"

"Yes. They are the very ancient tribes who inhabited Florida long before the Seminole arrived, so the legends go. Huge, hairy people who thrived in the swamps and beyond. Very secretive and to themselves. Supposed to be closer to the earth spirit, the primal forces behind it than the now so called Native Americans, and certainly the Europeans. It seems that all Native American cultures have very similar legends, which gave rise in the imaginations of the white man to the Sasquatch and Bigfoot myths, and down here the dumbest name of all, skunk ape ... because the Indians believed that these were real people of the earth, not some misplaced gorilla or giant monkey, not something destined for the endangered species list if one is ever verified or captured. They were, or are, people."

A curious smile of undivided attention on his face now, Sean asks, "Grandma told you this?"

"No. No. I learned that from research, background for a paper that Professor Griffin let me do for his zoology class. The purpose was to debunk those modern Bigfoot sightings, and other supposed evidence for their existence, on what he called 'sane and solid scientific grounds,' which I did, at least for him. I got an A minus." She raises her glass and tips it toward McDuff for an air toast. He follows. She proceeds with her tale.

"Now, my grandmother used to tell me that Palmetto Man, the Seminole lore version of Bigfoot, was still very much among us, that his race was the craftiest and most cunning people ever to roam the wilderness. Masters of stealth and secrecy. They could watch us, and later the white man, for long hours and learn about us, never revealing their presence. I guess they saw enough over the ages to learn that they wanted nothing to do with any of us."

"Sounds like they are awfully damn perceptive and intelligent too," Sean laughs. "I'll bet there's not a Republican among them."

Jane just laughs back softly and continues. There is a composure and a joy about her now that mystifies McDuff.

"She said that many times after her first encounter with one, after a while, that she would sit down cross legged under this or that tree and sort of converse. That is if one appeared, which was rare. She believed they had some psychic powers too, and they also had a very basic primitive language she began to notice. She tried to teach me some words, but I wasn't very good with foreign languages, or interested much back then. She did claim to have taught a couple of them the Muskogee Creek word for friend, *ahessi*, and that they learned to repeat it, and seemed to sense what it meant because grandma always greeted them with it when she came upon them, or when they came upon her. She would give them fish sometimes. They love fish."

Nothing witty can enter McDuff's mind now. He is suddenly a listener, too amazed to go back to the satire pool. He looks away for a moment and begins to connect the dots.

"That noise he made before he disappeared ... you know, it didn't seem to me like he was just making some wild animal noise. Yes ... it could have been ... hell, I'll bet it WAS ... a crude effort to return your ... well, greeting?"

"Anyway," Jane goes on, " a couple of weeks or so before my grandmother donned her magic beads, which she didn't always wear—a beautiful old thing of shells and turquoise, with a small gold pendant hanging from it—and walked off into the swamp to, well, meet her maker I guess they say, she told me that if I ever meet up with Palmetto Man that I should not show fear, and that I should say 'ahessi.'"

McDuff's eyes widen as he thinks, easy for grandma to say don't be afraid, especially when she's been hanging out with them for so many years. That was one huge, intimidating creature. Wisely he refrains from comment though, and Jane reaches across the table for his hand.

"Jane, what made you tell me to drop the machete, because instinctively it seems like disarming is the last thing you'd do when confronted by something like that?"

She squeezes his hand and lets go, then says, "Oh, that's another of grandma's details, and stories, that I flashed back to, almost immediately. She always insisted that the palmetto people were a very peaceful race, and that the only time they were known to be aggressive, the only time they were ever known to kill, is when their own lives were threatened. She said that through their secret observations of us they came to recognize Seminole and white man weapons, and were especially cautious when they saw them. She told me that the few tales in our tradition where the palmetto people killed warriors, or white men, were acts of self defense."

"That makes a lot of sense," Sean responds.

"I remember that she told me the story, twice, about some palmetto people who were very hungry and came upon a group of men who had just caught a lot of fish, and they just walked up to them and started taking the fish. Two warriors grabbed spears and one of them stabbed a Palmetto Man, but didn't hurt him much, and the hairy guys responded by decapitating two or three men with one swoop of their hands. When the others dropped their weapons the palmetto people just took a few more fish and disappeared."

"My god, that's a tough lesson to learn, but sure worth remembering,"

"So, you probably noticed that when you unsheathed the machete how the palmetto man took on a more aggressive posture?"

"Yes. Recall it well."

"Well," Jane slips off in thought momentarily, then adds, "It's amazing how this stuff just rushed back to me then and took over my thoughts. It's almost as if grandmother was standing there behind me whispering in my ear."

Jane takes a drink of water from the plastic bottle.

"I'm sorry," she says. "This must be awfully weird and boring."

"Absolutely not," he loudly returns. "Please tell me more, if you can. Really, Jane. I'm utterly astounded. Your remembering this so quickly probably saved our lives."

She grins and looks down into her glass of rum, then back up to Sean. Then a mild eureka sort of squint comes to her face. "You know, Sean." She pauses a few seconds to put her coming thoughts in order it seems. "Here's something that is going to sound really really strange."

"Don't stop my dear," he replies. "You are on a marvelous roll."

She looks down at her hands for a second, smiles and says OK, then continues. "Grandma always claimed that the palmetto people had a highly developed sense of smell, and that they could identify individuals, even families, by their singular odors, before even seeing them. Much more advanced I guess than any mammal's today. That was her theory. She said when she was in the presence of one and could see his or her face that at first the palmetto guy, or sometimes gal, would sniff a lot and seem to process what it took in very carefully."

"Hmmm," Sean interjects, now looking a little skeptical.

Jane notes his look and says, "So her convincing evidence of this is the time she lost one of her favorite bracelets in the swamp, after a morning pow-wow with a big male, who sat down across the clearing from her, and they sort of indulged in language lessons or something. This was maybe six or eight years into her very random encounters, maybe three or four a year, with the palmetto people. I guess they came to accept her as part of the fauna, and no threat."

"Yes," McDuff says, waiting for something resembling a punch line.

"Well grandmother was very upset at having lost the bracelet. General fatigue, and a lot of daily rains, kept her from going back to look for it. As if there was anything even close to a fat chance that she would find it. But!" Jane raises her right arm and extends her index finger. "Grandma claims that three days later she awoke early one morning and looked out her window, and there was the bracelet lying on her window sill."

Sean is slipping off into confusion now, not making a connection, and asks, "So, how do you think it turned up there?"

Jane laughs and says, "Well grandma claimed that one of her big hairy friends found and returned it, that he was able to, well, sniff her out. Plus she said that there were huge fresh footprints outside the window. Go figure."

"Whoa," McDuff remarks. "That's very unusual, isn't it."

She inhales deeply, exhales, sips on the water, then goes further. "Now. This is what occurred to me during our close encounter, when he disappeared without injuring or killing us. And after this crazy theory I have to go home to bed."

"No. No." Sean says sternly. "I insist you sleep here. The guest room is clean and ready to go. Fully equipped. Please. And I promise I won't try to hit on you. The door locks from the inside too."

She laughs and sighs, too tired to argue with his hospitality. "Deal," she replies. "Thank you so much, Sean. I really appreciate this." She rubs her eyes and gives it one more crazy reflection.

"When I was eight years old she took me with her on a day trip up into the wetlands, and those supposedly haunted sacred grounds northeast of the settlement. She said she wanted me to meet some friends, and you can probably figure by now what that meant. We walked for about an hour and I was getting pretty cranky and tired and bored, as I can recall, so we sat down in a small, clear area under some oaks and I promptly fell asleep in her lap for probably a full hour. When I awoke she told me I missed them, her friends ... that they came over to us and sniffed us for a minute or so, sort of smiled, then just slowly turned around and disappeared back into the hammocks."

McDuff is befuddled now, not following, and has to make his way back to the humor hot tub. "Well, that was pretty rude don't you think? I mean, they're the ones who are supposed to smell bad." Then he wonders, "So why didn't she wake you up? " Then it hits him: right, wake up your young granddaughter to see the monster. Bad timing. Bad idea. "Wait, nevermind," he says. "I think I know."

Jane laughs again and shakes her head, puts her face in her hands for a moment, and continues to throb with laughter. But when she looks up, there are tears streaming down her cheeks, which she is quick to explain to Sean are "tears of bewilderment and joy. Don't worry."

McDuff gets up from his chair and goes to Jane. She stands up to meet him and they put their arms around each other and hold on tight.

Jane is still laughing, and sobbing softly, when she says to Sean, "It is said that palmetto people live to be well over a hundred years old." Then she looks him in the eyes deeply. "Oh Sean, you know what I thought to myself tonight when he turned and vanished?"

"Tell me, darling. I swear I am not going to laugh at you, and we sure as hell can't tell anyone else this stuff."

She loosens her embrace, but maintains the arresting stare.

"I said ... seriously, I said to myself, 'I wonder if he remembered me?'"

18
Beyond Smithereens

Sean is awakened at nine a.m. by a light tap on his bedroom door.

"Sean?"

"Jane ... good morning. I'll be right there."

"It's OK ...listen, I'm sorry but I just got a voicemail on my cell, from my sister, and she is taking mother to the emergency room ... and I need to get over there to meet them."

"Oh damn it Jane, I'm so sorry, again. Hold on while I throw some clothes on."

"OK. Meet me outside."

He quickly puts on shorts and t-shirt, and slips on his Topsiders. When he gets to the front porch Jane is standing by her SUV, door open and engine running. She runs over to meet him halfway down the walk and they hug. Then McDuff asks, "Does it sound serious?"

"I don't think so, but Nel doesn't want to take any chances it sounds like." Jane kisses him on the lips, then says again that she's sorry. They hug again.

"I understand Jane. It'll be OK I'm sure. Call me when you can, and let me know how she is, and how you are, all right?"

"Of course I will. As soon as I can. I promise. We have a lot more to talk about." She releases him, turns and starts for the car, then turns back and rushes up to hug him again. He holds her tight and rocks her softly back and forth.

"Oh damn it," she exclaims. "You know, in spite of the bizarre ingredients, last night was one of the best nights of my life."

Mac grins and says, "Ditto my darling. Get back here as soon as you can. I have to know more about my woodland neighbor to the north."

"And there's a lot more things about my former professor that I want to know."

She whirls and skips to her car, gets in and closes the door, backs it up and turns it around, heads down the driveway and out the access road.

Sean waves as she disappears around the first stand of live oaks. An odd snippet of a favorite musical lyric comes to his lips, "... leavin' like a gypsy queen in a fairytale."

As Jane pulls out on to the county road to head south she asks herself, "Do I really want to go away to graduate school?"

Over the next few days life for Sean and Jane maintains a fine, happy simmer. She phones him early Sunday evening to report that her mother is back in the hospital with a mild relapse of pneumonia. Her doctor says they are keeping her until they are absolutely sure they have squashed the bug this time. They believe Mrs. Kowechobe will recover nicely. It's a relief for all. On the down side, Jane's sister reveals that she is going through a divorce, having caught her husband with another woman. The affair has been going on for months. What irks Nel most is that the other woman is one of many Disney employees who wears the big Mickey Mouse costume every evening during the parade at Magic Kingdom, and she's not even the best Mickey, Nel feels. So, in the wake of this family tsunami, and utter exhaustion, Jane Green tells Mac she won't be coming to his place until late Monday afternoon, if it's all right. It's absolutely all right, he tells her. He will make a much needed supplies run to town in the afternoon, and he will cook dinner. Jane says she is flattered and impressed.

After a light Monday lunch McDuff relaxes on the deck with a glass of iced tea. The joys and jostles of the previous forty-eight hours zip back and forth across his mind's eye, as if he's watching a jar filled with fireflies on speed. Even the recollection of those first face-to-face seconds with the Palmetto Man raises a smile. He wonders why he didn't go into horrified shock and stay there. Maybe because of Jane, he tells himself. I wanted to protect Jane more than anything else. But that's only ye olde tip of the iceberg it seems. That beast, that creature ... he was .... Mac slides into English major mode for a moment and recalls a paper he did in grad school on the religious dimensions of *Moby-Dick*. Some critic, or maybe a theologian, describes Ishmael's initial reaction to the sight of the great white whale as not so much a moment of common, blinding fear as one of "respectful dread," like the attitude of the Old Testament Israelites toward Yahweh. Something like scary awe, with extreme caution. So, you can let it derange you and kill you, or you can just hang on, pay attention, and see what happens. So there are more things in heaven, and earth, Horatio ... yada yada yada.

McDuff reaches for the glass and takes a sip of the chilly green tea. He sits the drink back on the table, frowns, and slaps himself lightly on the right cheek.

"Holy mackerel," he declares softly to the river flowing by him. "Barry was on to something a while back when he said that maybe I need to get a life." Screw literary scholarship here, he thinks. I'll never be able to explain it, even if I could tell the story to anyone.

When Jane arrives the following afternoon she looks remarkable, and recovered. Two days featuring green blazing vandalism, cryptozoological adventure, and family worries are not showing. She and Sean relax on the deck, sipping lemonade and reliving, rehashing, reacting in retrospect, to the boom and the beast. On the topic of the palmetto man, Sean finds relief in Jane's recollection of another common element of Native American lore concerning the nature of the fellow: its other names, Man Mountain, Windigo, Sand People, Elder Brother imply something more mystical than monstrous. In fact, Jane remembers that the appearance of Bigfoot, or Palmetto Man, is often thought to be a sign of approaching good fortune, or a caution to mend your ways in order to reap blessings. So it's very unlikely, Sean thinks, that one will bust in here, rip off my head, and lumber off with the salmon fillets in the freezer. That is, if Saturday night was all real in the first place.

Is it possible, he wonders, that one of the yet unknown side effects, or fallouts, of that new experimental explosive is a temporary element in the surrounding air, produced by the violent chemical reactions, that induces hallucinations! Old hippies will want to know.

As for the bombing itself, Jane tells Sean, "You should see the site now."

It startles him to think that she went back for a look. But the fear quickly ends when she goes on to say that she was able to pull it up on Google Earth/Daily Planet, plus another semiprivate Air Force app with greater visual and magnification capabilities. Praise satellites.

"All you can see is a charred crater probably eighty feet across," she reports. "My guess is that it's ten to fifteen feet deep at the center, and there is literally not a scrap of machinery to be seen. Vaporized mostly, I'm sure, maybe a few small, mangled and unidentifiable pieces scattered over the landscape. It's good that Polly was between us and the heavy equipment or we might have found some of it in our laps. When the local authorities see this I'll wager that the first thing they'll think is 'asteroid.'"

Sean and Jane go on to enjoy a dinner of theoretically fresh tilapia, baked potatoes, mixed vegetables, and coleslaw. Bottle of cabernet. Key Lime pie.

But the deliciously fated dessert comes around midnight, strong and sweet beyond any anticipations. They become lovers.

———————

Jane leaves by midmorning of the next day to visit her mother at the hospital, and to take her sister to lunch. She tells McDuff that she will return with dinner. On the road to the hospital she tells herself that she is not, as the saying goes, happy as a clam, for clams can have no idea. She's much more elated than anything can know.

Similarly Sean, strolling out to the river's edge now for a short nature walk, recalls the closing lines of one of his favorite poems, Roethke's "Words for the Wind," and says out loud, "... I dance round and round, A fond and foolish man, And see and suffer myself /In another being at last." He runs his fingers down the right side of his smiling face and thinks, finally the whole darn poem makes sense to me. Then he frowns, slaps himself in the face once more and thinks, there I go again.

At four in the afternoon his phone rings and it's Jane, very excited.

"Sean! Sean!

"Yes Jane, how's your mother?"

"Oh thanks, she's doing great, but you won't believe this!"

"What?"

"Oh Sean, I got the scholarship! Gulf Coast is giving me a free ride! Can you believe it?"

He lights up inside and out and wishes she was there right now to embrace. "Oh Jane, hell yes I believe it. Yes! Congratulations love. How did, or when, did you find out?"

"I got a phone call from the Dean a few hours ago."

"I am so happy for you, but no, not surprised at all. You are more than deserving. It's great news."

"Oh Sean, I could almost cry. I'm so happy. And mom is too. I think this news is going to take a couple of days off her hospital stay. You should have seen how happy she was. Even my sister."

"Well my dearest, I should be cooking you dinner again. And I will break out my remaining bottle of really good bubbly, and rum if we need it. Where are you now?"

"I'm just about to leave my place. Then I'm stopping at Loozy-ann's for a big take-out of their seafood gumbo, and that good bread. Have you had it?"

"Good choice, yes."

"I'll be there in less than and hour, and I love you." Click.

McDuff is watching for Jane's arrival, and when she pulls into the driveway he hurries out to greet her with a big hug and a kiss. They head to the kitchen, Jane with gumbo bucket and bread in hands.

"Think we need to nuke this gumbo a little to warm it up," Sean asks as he relieves her of the food.

"Oh, maybe a minute would help," is Jane's reply.

Dinner is loud with celebration. In a half hour they reduce the bottle of Veuve Clicquot by two thirds. Jane notices the small flat-screen TV on the opposite wall and says, "Hey darling, you know I haven't read a paper or seen the news in three days. Let's turn it on and see if our friend Polly has gotten anyone's attention."

"That's not a bad idea, love." He gets up and retrieves the remote, pulls his chair over next to Jane and flicks on the television. "Did you bring any popcorn," he smiles and asks. She giggles.

It's CNN, so Sean says that maybe they should try the local channels. But quickly he sits the remote on the table when a bearded bespectacled anchorman says, "Very big news out of south Florida today following a tremendous explosion near the Everglades late Saturday night that destroyed a construction site and numerous pieces of heavy equipment. For a detailed update we switch you now to our correspondent, Leann Collingsworth, on the scene near Rivercrest, Florida."

"Thank you, Delbert. Authorities here are mum on details as to what may have caused the blast Saturday that literally obliterated a construction site just north of here, totally destroying, we are told, three large bulldozers, two multi-ton dump trucks and a modular office trailer, all owned by M.C. Bodey Enterprises, one of the state's largest and sometimes most controversial developers."

"Delbert, local law enforcement tells us that when they were called to the scene Sunday morning by employees of the company they were simply aghast over what they saw." She begins to read from note cards. "A deep hundred-feet wide crater is practically all that remains, and a few variously mangled, unidentifiable pieces of steel are scattered in the surrounding woods. Delbert, my sources say that it looks like the aftermath of a small nuclear explosion, but no radioactivity has been detected. So thank god for that."

"Leeann, has there been any speculation as to who or what may have caused this then?"

"That's the unnerving part of this, Del. Yesterday morning the FBI was brought in, and by noon, I am told they had called in the CIA. While no one on the various investigating teams is talking yet, and no press conference is scheduled for the near future, the speculation is that this is snowballing into a very serious issue relating to national security, hence the growing involvement of the CIA. Local authorities have in fact been removed from the investigation, and all routes in and out of the blast scene have been roped off for a mile in every direction. Armed guards from a local U.S. Army Reserves unit have been called in and posted at the perimeters of this very unnerving crime scene. Coast Guard patrol boats have been dropped by helicopter into the Cypress River, which borders the site."

"That indeed sounds like a delicate, serious situation. What else can you tell us right now, Leeann?"

"Well Delbert, one federal agent close to the investigation, who requires anonymity at this point, speculates that the explosive that was employed is a very powerful and guarded experimental substance that is a top secret and classified element in America's military arsenal. If this substance has fallen into the hands of nonmilitary personnel, it represents a very dangerous threat to national security."

"Oh my, Leeann. Does this mean that terrorism is suspected here?"

"No Delbert, although terrorism has not been completely ruled out. It seems unlikely that terrorists would target a construction site in the middle of nowhere. Most likely a more public and visual target would have been sought. No witnesses have come forward, but that's not surprising given the sparsely populated surrounding area. The closest residences are at least five miles away, and on the night of the explosion, violent thunderstorms were moving across the region."

Sean and Jane are wide-eyed and mouths agape now, although smiles are trying to form on their faces. The reporter on the television is handed a sheet of paper from someone off screen. She looks down for a few seconds, then continues.

"Del, this breaking news has just been handed to me. The CIA has taken into custody for questioning, four people; the owner of Bodey Enterprises, one Mr. M.C. Bodey, along with three of his associates and employees. As we speak they are being transported to McDill Air Force base in Tampa, where they will be flown to Washington and a meeting with Pentagon officials."

"Yes! Yes!" Jane is jumping for joy now. McDuff joins her, and they prance about the kitchen.

"Oh Jane," Sean says. "Couldn't happen to a better person. Oh my goodness, I sure didn't see that coming, did you?"

Jane admits, it crossed her mind that Bodey might have a world of explaining to do if the feds get wind and figure out that A40 is involved. But the intrigue and emotions of the past few days overpowered any further speculation. She mostly cares about getting to know better the new man in her world, about finally getting her life on a track that is not up hill only, and riddled with needless speed bumps. She relishes it, a place in life now where she doesn't have to be watching over her shoulder for another officer bent on pinching her ass.

This is the beginning of the end for Bodey, Sean believes. Even the Tallahass Ass cannot keep him in the fold in the wake of this very suspicious incident. The government may not be able to prosecute in the end, if there is an end, but there is certainly dirt here that will never wash off. The college will benefit, the Glades are safer for a while longer, and the Seminoles can maybe feel that the Great Spirit has blessed them with a minor victory. And Jane. Lovely, wondrous Jane. McDuff is sure that, under the circumstances, his lost Sarah approves. Testimony to the advice from the old Appalachian philosopher she liked to quote: "Don't turn yer back on life, jess like you shouldn' turn yer back on some suspected culprit slinkin' 'roun' behind you." Not exactly optimism, or pessimism, but something like good survival skills.

The new lovers laugh and hug through the midnight hour. Some future scenarios are entertained. Jane may move in with Sean for the summer, as her lease expires at the end of the month. And since Nel is moving in with mother, the sister can help a lot at the family shop too. As for graduate school (and you ARE going to grad school Sean tells her) they will make it work. Whether McDuff is long for Cypress State? Maybe. Maybe not. He may have a bestseller or two in his soul that is ready to hatch. Why not?

———

When morning sifts brightly through Sean's bedroom window shades, the lovers are naked in each other's arms. Not a lot of sleep, but what there is of it is sound and peaceful, save for a faint, brief clatter outside, around four a.m., coming from the area of the big potted frangipani off the end of the deck. McDuff imagines raccoons, a possum, a silly armadillo perhaps, just passing through.

They get up and shower together. Dress. Shorts and tank tops for both.

Sean cooks eggs over easy, some veggie bacon strips by Morning Star Farms, wheat bread toast, cubed honeydew and cantaloupe, milk and OJ.

"Do you mind if I think of you as a keeper," Jane playfully asks.

"Keep it up," he replies, feigning a grumpy tone.

"Oh, I think you love it, my professor."

"It? It? No, I do not love IT, my dearest. I love YOU."

Jane smiles and shakes her head, then leans over and kisses his cheek.

They finish breakfast, then move outside and settle into lounge chairs facing the river. For no reason it seems, Sean remembers the noise that briefly awakened him in the middle of the night and glances to his left, over to the frangipani, which to his surprise is all ready sporting a few yellow flowers, thanks in part to a very mild winter. He notices a faint glitter coming off of something lying on the flagstone next to the pot. Crow, raven, or maybe mockingbird stash he thinks, what the heck. He gets up to take a look. Jane's eyes follow him.

He stoops down, and to his surprise it's a string of dirty, faded white beads; a tarnished round pendant of sorts, about the size of a half-dollar, dangles from the rotting leather string that is barely keeping it all together. He scoops it all into the palm of his right hand and walks back to Jane. He bends down and shows it to her and asks, with a puzzled frown, "This isn't yours, is it?"

The brightness of the late morning sun makes it difficult for her to focus immediately, and she places her right hand above her eyes to shade them. Then she gasps. She carefully takes it from Sean's outstretched hands, gets up quickly and walks to the edge of the deck to the railing. Sean slowly follows.

Jane looks intently at the old and worn string of tiny shells, coquina, some turquoise, now in her left hand, then she speaks sternly to McDuff. "Sean, please don't joke with me now, OK." Gently she moves the beads away from the pendant and turns it over. There is a crude etching of a turtle, or a tortoise. The other side is blank. She begins to breathe more deliberately as she stares into Sean's eyes with a desperately serious scrutiny.

"Sean, please tell me, truthfully. Where did you get this?"

He can see now that she is teetering on some strange, thin emotional cliff, with wild chaos below. Or is it? A warm panic grips him.

I've never in my life wanted to say the right thing more than I do now, he tells himself.

"Honestly Jane," he finally gets out. "I just remembered hearing something out there, in the middle of the night, some little thing and I thought raccoons or something. And for some reason I just thought to look over there, and noticed something a little shiny, and ... you saw me, I just went over there to see what it was."

The stern glare begins to fade from Jane's face and eyes. A glimmer of relief comes to Sean's. "Jane. Jane," he says, some wavering in his voice. "Are you all right? I mean, I'm really sorry. But what is it?"

She closes her hand on the beads, but the pendant hangs out, reflecting sunlight. Jane puts her arms around McDuff and says, "Oh Sean. I apologize for the dramatics again, really." She kisses his lips, then backs up, holding her left hand head high, then says, "Oh Sean. Everything has been so intense, and fast, and so wonderful these last few weeks."

She looks down, moving her head side to side as her long gleaming hair falls across her chest. A short laugh bursts from her and she shakes her fist containing the beads. The dangling pendant seems to be coming alive.

"Oh Sean!" She shakes her hand more intensely, as if invoking, conjuring, then looks over McDuff's shoulder for an instant, as if expecting a visitor. She laughs again, a sad but happy laugh, and says, "Oh Sean, this is my grandma's magic necklace!"

Made in the USA
Charleston, SC
17 January 2014